To Dick
What a great mentor!
Keep up with your
writing. I hope
to have a copy
of your book
some day.

Tonya Jean
McGue

Running Home
A Quest for Answers

Tonya Jean McGue

Bloomington, IN Milton Keynes, UK

authorHOUSE™

AuthorHouse™
1663 Liberty Drive, Suite 200
Bloomington, IN 47403
www.authorhouse.com
Phone: 1-800-839-8640

AuthorHouse™ *UK Ltd.*
500 Avebury Boulevard
Central Milton Keynes, MK9 2BE
www.authorhouse.co.uk
Phone: 08001974150

First published by AuthorHouse   7/3/2006

ISBN: 1-4259-4069-2 (sc)

Library of Congress Control Number: 2006904924

Printed in the United States of America
Bloomington, Indiana

This book is printed on acid-free paper.

*AUTHOR'S NOTE: This is a work of fiction. Names, characters, places
and incidents are either the product of the author's imagination or are
used fictitiously, and any resemblance to actual persons, living or dead,
business establishments, events, or locales is entirely coincidental.*

*To my grandmother Donna Bryan
and in memory
of my grandmother Hazel Berkley*

ACKNOWLEDGMENTS

I'd like to thank Floyd Kemske and Shannon McGue for their excellent editing; author Walter Wangerin Jr. for providing inspiration and guidance; proofreaders Peggy Nelson, Tracey Pickford and John McGue; my parents Tom and Sharon Berkley for their encouragement; and most of all, my loving and supportive husband and children.

Chapter 1

Melinda sat in the silence of what had been her mother's room. She slumped against the wall, staring at the chipped, silver doorknob. Her eyes roamed around the room until they rested for a moment on the half open window and the thin billowy curtains, reaching toward her. The wooden floor was scattered with dust balls and tiny crumbled pieces of paper and a single earring, long and skinny and shining in the light from the window. The cool, empty room made her body shudder, but she didn't notice and left her crumpled sweater on her lap.

She breathed in the salty ocean breezes that drifted in and lingered, so familiar. The smell was as common to her as the sound she now listened to, children laughing and screaming beyond the window. So much was the same, but so much was different.

Melinda imagined the children running in the nearby sand. She was young not so long ago. She played with her mother on that same beach. Her thoughts drifted. Her mother held both her hands and twirled her small body around and around. Melinda remembered her mother's feet making tiny circles in the sand; her tan toes gripping the soft surface. Their world surrounded them again and again. From her rotating position, Melinda glimpsed the ocean, enormous jutting rocks, families on the beach and shoreline cottages. As her mother turned faster, the scenes blurred into warm colors. Melinda shrieked with excitement, returning her mother's smile. Her bare legs waved behind her. Her mother slowed, staggered and then they both fell spread-eagle on the sand as the clouds above continued to spin.

A tap on the door stole Melinda's memory away. She turned toward the door where Darcy stood as if she were afraid to enter.

"Mel?"

"Yeah."

"Are you all right?"

"Yeah."

"I'm going to make some spaghetti, your favorite," Darcy said. "Would you like some? I think it would be good for you to eat before you leave."

Leave. The word hung in the air in front of both of them.

Melinda watched the floating curtains again. They reminded her of dancers. Hadn't her mother been a dancer when she was young? Melinda thought she recalled that, but wasn't certain. Now, the curtains twirled toward the middle of the room, toward Melinda.

"If spaghetti doesn't sound good, Mel, we could go out to eat. Does that sound better?" Darcy stepped slowly across the room. "We could go to The Loft. You could say goodbye to everyone before you go."

Before I go. Why does she have to keep saying those words? Soon, we'll both be gone. Our house will be empty.

Through the window, past the curtains, she watched a cluster of clouds racing over the green roof of Mack's Hardware Store. The sun was setting and the children's voices were gone. The store door banged across the street. Mack was leaving, closing time. Melinda's mom used to say she could set her clock by the closing of the hardware store. Melinda had watched Mack leave the store a hundred times before. Now, in her head she pictured his movements. Mack's big key chain jangled beneath his thick, callused fingers. When he finally found the right one, he locked the door before dangling the whole bunch onto his left belt loop. He reached into his overalls and pulled out his pack of Skoal. After tucking a big wad under his front lip, he turned to walk the three blocks home. When her mother was alive, Mack often looked toward their house. If he saw Melinda, he winked. If he saw her mother, he shyly waved and said, "Hey, Carole." Her mother smiled and returned the greeting, "Hey, Mack." Then he walked home with a big grin on his face.

Melinda liked Mack. He'd given her bubble gum as long as she could remember. When she was younger, she used to hint to her mother that she thought he'd make a pretty good daddy to some child, somewhere, someday. Last year, when Melinda was thirteen, she'd gotten the nerve up to ask her mother why she never dated. Her mother said she was too busy working and when she wasn't working, she wanted to spend time with her.

Darcy stood very close now with her arm extended and her hand near Melinda's face. Darcy's nails were always painted. Melinda stared at the chipped burgundy polish.

"Come on, I'll help you up," Darcy urged. "Your bottom's probably sore from this old, hard floor. It's chilly in here too. I'll shut the window."

"No," Melinda yelled. Her voice echoed in the empty room. Softer, she said. "I want it open, and I want to stay right here as long as I can."

"I know you do," Darcy said, almost under her breath. "Okay. I have an idea. I'll order us spaghetti from The Loft. We'll eat right here. How does that sound? Then you don't have to leave yet and I can get you to eat something, hopefully. You know you haven't finished packing."

Melinda was silent.

"Do you want me to do it for you? There are only a few more things to throw in the bags."

Melinda nodded.

"Okay. I'll be in the other room if you need me."

Melinda watched Darcy leave. She and her mother had been best friends and waitresses together at The Loft. Darcy knew Melinda almost as well as her mother. She had been there the day Melinda was born 14 years ago, helped walk her to school on her first day of kindergarten and stayed with her when her mother flew home for her grandfather's funeral. Melinda wanted to go too, but they could barely afford one ticket. Darcy had loaned her mother $100 to help pay for the airfare to Chicago.

"I put your bags by the door." Darcy was standing in the room again. "I didn't know where to put your brush so I decided to put it in your backpack to take on the airplane. I thought you might want to brush your hair before you get off the plane to meet your uncle. It's in the side pocket. Okay?"

Melinda shrugged.

"Mel, please talk to me."

Melinda continued to stare out the window at the darkening sky.

"I can't stand this silence anymore. You and your mother were the strong ones, not me." Darcy hesitated, let out a big sigh and slumped forward. "I don't know what to do. I miss your mother too. I can't imagine life without her either. . . and now you're leaving. I'm afraid I'll never see you again." Darcy began to cry. "Oh, please Mel, talk to me before you go. I don't think I could stand it if you didn't."

Melinda stared at the torn buckles on Darcy's sandals. Her toenail polish was chipped too, except it was pink not burgundy.

Darcy took a deep breath and turned to walk out of the room.

"Don't go," Melinda whispered. "Please don't go."

Darcy wiped a tear from her cheek and turned back toward Melinda.

"I was just thinking about the last thing my mom said to me," Melinda said with a far away look, clutching the sweater on her lap. "I was on my way out to meet Brenda and Susan. We were going to the first football game of the season. Do you know what she said?"

Melinda looked up. Darcy's shoulder-length, black hair was a mess, her eyes were puffy and mascara was smeared down her rouge-covered cheeks. Darcy seemed tall, but Melinda knew if she stood up, she towered over her temporary guardian. Darcy used to tease Melinda about passing her in height, but Melinda knew it would eventually happen. Darcy was only five feet one inch. Melinda had passed her during her seventh grade year and was now 5' 6", the same height as her mother.

"What did your mother say to you?" Darcy put her back to the wall and slid down next to Melinda. Once settled, she reached for Melinda's hand and caressed the tops of her fingers. Melinda sat Indian style. Darcy stretched next to her. Melinda glanced at the familiar clothing Darcy wore almost daily, baggy jeans and floppy sandals. The brown leather was scratched and faded and one of the top buckles was broken.

"What did she say, Mel?"

Melinda took a deep breath and began to talk slowly.

"I had just taken a big bite out of an apple. She came into the kitchen. She had on her biking shorts and I knew she was going for a ride. She handed me this," Melinda said. She pulled her sweater up to her chest and held it tight. "She said, 'It's getting chilly.' I rolled my eyes at her, put my apple on the counter and tied the sweater around my waist. I said, 'I'll take it, but I'm not going to wear it. This is my favorite shirt. I'm not covering it up.' Mom said, 'When it gets cold later, you'll be glad you have it.' She kissed me right here, grinned and said, 'What would you do without me?'"

Melinda swallowed hard, turning her face away from Darcy. She lifted the sweater to her cheek and felt the softness against her skin.

"I said, 'Just be a little cold I guess,'" Melinda whispered.

Darcy put her arm around Melinda's shoulder and pulled her close. Melinda looked down at the dark and light grain patterns in the wood. Her eyes followed the waves in and out from her feet all the way to the other side of the room. She glanced out the window again, but everything was dark now.

"What a dumb thing to say," Melinda said.

"No, it wasn't," Darcy said and then sniffled. In the last week, Darcy cried every time someone mentioned Carole. Hearing Darcy cry wasn't something new to Melinda. Darcy was the most sentimental person she knew. Melinda remembered her mom's friend crying when she lost her first tooth, when she learned how to ride a bike, and even when Melinda brought home her first report card with all A's.

Melinda took a deep breath, exhaling long and slow. She cupped her face in her hands and felt her cold fingertips on her forehead. Darcy squeezed her a little tighter. Melinda noticed their bodies rising and lowering together.

"I didn't know it would be the last time I saw her," Melinda said.

"Of course you didn't," Darcy said, crying louder. "Oh, honey, it doesn't seem like it now, but everything will be okay." She stroked Melinda's hair over and over. "I'm so glad you are talking. I was so worried. You haven't said five words since the accident. Lord, I can't stop crying. I'm sorry."

Melinda felt Darcy trembling.

Since the accident, everyone told her it was okay, even good, to cry. She tried to cry now. She wanted in to her mother's room with Darcy. But she felt empty. Nothing came out. She couldn't even muster up a tear.

• • •

A few minutes later, Melinda listened as Darcy answered a knock on the front door. From her spot on the floor, she could hear Mr. Kolton describing the food he was delivering from The Loft. She heard him tell Darcy that it's "on the house." The sweet smell of garlic bread and spaghetti made her stomach gurgle. She hadn't eaten more than a few nibbles in days.

Mr. Kolton whispered, "How's she doing?" For a second, Melinda thought about saying, "It's a small house. I can hear you," but nothing came out of her mouth. This past week, she had preferred to keep all her thoughts to herself.

She listened to Darcy's answer. "Better, I think. She started talking a few minutes ago."

"Good luck at the airport," he said. "Give her my love and best wishes, will ya?"

"Sure, Mr. Kolton. Thanks for the food. I'll see you at work tomorrow."

"It will be good to have you back," he said. "See you tomorrow."

They ate out of Styrofoam boxes on the floor of her mother's room by the light of a single lamp Darcy brought from the living room.

"Did you know that Mr. Kolton and Mack are heading up a committee to get Highway 101 widened?" Darcy said. "They're trying to get a big shoulder put in with a yellow stripe and all. It will have its own lane just for bikers and runners. It's about time."

Darcy held her box up under her mouth. She said, "Mmmmm. This is so good."

Melinda always marveled at how Darcy ate. She got so much pleasure from it.

She didn't answer Darcy's question. She knew where the conversation would lead and didn't want to talk about her mother or the accident anymore.

"Now is a good time to get something like that done. People will listen more after a bad accident," Darcy said. "It needed to be done a long time ago."

Melinda was trying to think about something else.

"It will be much safer," Darcy said, wrapping spaghetti around her fork. "No one else will get hurt or killed." Her words faded off and the last word was barely a whisper.

Melinda put her food down and looked at the far corner of the room. Spider webs zigzagged from one corner to the next. She noticed the dark marks and smudges on the bare walls. The room hadn't been painted in years.

"I'm sorry," Darcy said. "I guess you don't really want to talk about that."

Melinda shook her head. She was trying hard to get the reoccurring images out of her head. But they lingered. She saw her mother riding her bike down the highway, her head low and her legs pumping. Then she saw the weaving, speeding car. *Mom watch out*, her thoughts always screamed, but the words never made any difference.

They ate without talking for a while and then Darcy said, "I'm cold. Do you mind if I shut the window?"

Melinda shook her head and watched Darcy walk across the room. Before, she would have had to go all the way around the bed to get to the window, but now it was a straight shot.

"Where's all our furniture?" Melinda said.

Darcy grunted and pushed down on the cracked, wooden frame. "Oh, this is so hard to shut." She inched the window all the way to the bottom, pushing on one side and then the other. The curtains fell still against the wall.

"I put everything in storage at that place on the south end of town. I'll keep it there for you. When you get older and get a place of your own, you may want it."

"I don't think so," Melinda said.

"Well, I'll keep it for a while just in case."

Melinda finished the last of her spaghetti and shut the lid.

"What about the house?" she said.

Darcy took a deep breath and let out a long sigh.

"Well, the Porters are real interested in it. They're getting ready to have a baby, you know, and their house has only one bedroom. Having two would be very nice for them. Don't you think?"

Melinda didn't answer. The thought of someone else in the only house she'd ever known was almost unbearable. She felt angry. Why did this have to happen? Why was her mother taken away from her? She hated the thought of leaving. This was her life. Her friends were here.

Darcy continued, "So, I thought maybe we could sell it to them. The money would go into your trust fund for when you turn 21."

"Stop. Stop. Stop," Melinda yelled. "Don't say anything else. I don't want to hear about anything." She glared at Darcy and then turned away.

After a few minutes, Darcy stood and Melinda knew it was time to go.

Chapter 2

Melinda stood next to Darcy's rusty Volkswagen Beetle, peering over the top at her house for the last time. Her eyes stopped on the orange glow of the porch light, the one that her mother always left on so Melinda could get in safely. As Darcy started the car, Melinda whispered, "I'm sorry. I didn't mean to yell at you."

Darcy just nodded and backed out of the driveway. Melinda scanned the scene. Even in the dark, she saw every detail. Only a block from the wide Pacific Ocean, her little dead end street was lined on one side with five white, single story homes. Her short gravel driveway stopped on the left side of the house where a mended concrete porch led to their small kitchen. She'd recently started cooking and was pleased to have a meal ready when her mother came home from a long day at the restaurant. The living room was only big enough for a sofa, chair and television.

She and her mother liked to read together on the sofa. Two bedrooms with a bathroom in between squared off the house. The yard was small, but big enough for Melinda and her friends to play. Grass grew patchy in the sandy soil where occasionally they would discover a shell or a unique fossil rock. Paint peeled off the white exterior of the house and the yellow trim, of which her mother was especially proud, now paled to an almost off-white. She could still hear her mother saying, "Everything either fades or rusts when you live near the sea, but it's a small price to pay for living in paradise, and I'd never live any other place."

Across the street, Mack's Hardware Store took up the entire block. Mack Sr. built the original store some 30 years ago and now his son Mack Jr. ran it. Mack's backed up to Phil's One-Stop Gas Station and Convenience Store that faced Highway 101. Highway 101 ran smack down the middle of Shorewood Beach, Oregon. Snake Highway, as the locals called it, meandered in and out of the jutting Western coastline, all the way from Washington to California. If you wanted to go for a long bike ride or run, Highway 101 was the route with the least stops especially after you got out of town a ways. The short blocks and grid-like pattern of Shorewood Beach's streets were hard to run on, and the beach was barricaded by jutting rocks, so Melinda and her mother often biked and ran together on Snake Highway.

The only stoplight in Shorewood Beach stood like a beacon at the corner of Highway 101 and Main Street. Melinda remembered when the light went up. She was in the second grade and her class took a field trip to watch it be turned on for the first time. Little shops and restaurants lined Main Street all the way from Third Avenue to the beach. Melinda bragged to her mother once that she knew every crack in every sidewalk in the entire town. This was her town, the entire eleven blocks north and south and the five blocks east and west.

The beach was her backyard. *Travel Magazine* declared it "One of the 10 most beautiful beaches in the world." Mountainous rocks darting in and out of view lined the broad sandy shore. Waves crashed into the giant rocks, flew upward and then splashed back into the ocean, leaving a lingering cool mist in the air. Tourists came from all over the world just to take pictures of the famous Sally's Rock. It was one of the most popular scenes on calendars, posters and inspirational verses.

During low tide, the tidal pools that formed between the rocks were one of Melinda's favorite places. The warm pools were a welcome refuge from the cold Pacific waves. Crabs also liked the warm water and scurried along the rocks to soak up the sun. Local children learned to watch out for the little pinchers at a young age.

Melinda now stuck her head out the window and listened to the sound of the water. Low tide, she thought. Darcy made the big curve to the east off of Snake Highway and onto 46. Melinda looked past Darcy and between the passing porch lights and caught a glimpse of Barker School. She'd gone there since kindergarten. She would have started eighth grade next week. Now, Susan and Brenda would go on without her.

As the school faded from sight, Darcy broke the silence.

"You know I'll have my car paid off in a few months and then I'm going to start saving money so I can come visit you. I've never been on an airplane. Your mom used to say that downtown Chicago was a fun place. I've heard it has lots of good restaurants. They say taxis jam the streets, always honking." Darcy laughed. "Maybe we could even ride in a taxi. That would be another first for me. What about you? Do you think it would be fun to go downtown? Ride in a taxi?"

Melinda shrugged. Her mind was still at home, not on some far away place she'd never been and didn't want to go. They drove into the thick trees of the Oregon National Forest.

"Why can't I stay here with you?" Melinda asked even though she knew the answer. Darcy had explained it to her. She legally had to live with her next of kin, even if she didn't know him.

"You know I'd love that. I hate this as much as you do Mel."

"When can I come back?"

"Well, I don't know. Maybe next summer. Maybe even for a whole week."

"A week's not long," Melinda interrupted. She tried to control her anger because she knew it wasn't Darcy's fault, but she also couldn't control how she felt.

She was back to not wanting to talk about anything. She stared out the window, watching the tops of the evergreens and the roll of the mountain ridges in the distance.

Her eyes ached. She slouched down in the seat and closed them.

When Melinda awoke, they were in the Portland airport parking garage. She arched her back, stretched out her arms and yawned. She looked over at Darcy who was sitting with her hands folded in her lap.

"I want to be strong for you right now, Mel. I always wished I was more like Carole," she began. "She was so strong. You remind me of her when I first met her. She was 18 or 19. She'd just arrived in Shorewood from that Chicago suburb, Belle Meade or something fancy like that. She didn't know a soul. She was striking. Earthy, but sophisticated. Flawless skin and long, thick hair. Not an ounce of make-up on. You could tell she came from a home with a lot of money, but she never acted snobby a day in her life that I know of. She was such a natural beauty. And there I was, kind of embarrassed like, with three shades of eye shadow, bright orange lipstick and long fake nails. I had just graduated from high school and thought I was hot stuff, until I saw the likes of her."

Darcy laughed. "Makes me wonder now how we ever became friends. She watched everything she ate. Only ate healthy. Me, I ate chips and cookies and, of course, my favorite, brownie a-la-mode with extra chocolate sauce." Darcy smiled at Melinda. "Anyways, your mother walked into The Loft with a duffle bag slung over her shoulder. I could see right away that she was a confident gal. She said to Mr. Kolton, 'I need a job and then I need to know where to look for a place to live.' She had a poncho on so I didn't notice that she was pregnant at first. Her belly wasn't that big anyway, even though she was six months pregnant. We were short a waitress so Mr. Kolton hired her right on the spot. After she left, I ran out on the sidewalk and told her she might want to check out the house for sale right around the corner. I told her they'd probably give her a good price because it needed a lot of fixin' up." Darcy looked at Melinda again. "That was your house."

She continued, "Later, she told me about leaving home and travelin' across the country. She'd stopped and worked at restaurants all along the way. Stayed in cheap motels and youth hostels. She had enough to put a down payment on your place. I admired Carole from the day I met her. I couldn't have asked for a better friend. I used to always tell her I wished I could change this or that about myself, but she always said she liked me just the way I was, even if I was a little crazy and insecure at sometimes."

Darcy put her hands over her face and began sobbing. "She liked me for me, for who I was, just the way I am," Darcy said. "I'm sorry I keep crying Mel."

Darcy was always saying sorry about something. Melinda had heard her mother tell Darcy that she didn't have to apologize all the time.

"It's okay," Melinda finally said.

They walked from the dim garage, through the bright airport, all the way to the gate in silence. Just before Melinda boarded the airplane, Darcy held Melinda's hands and stared at her face for a long time.

"Mel, I know you're trying to be strong and I know I apologize for crying so much, but it's good to cry sometimes. It makes me feel better. I told you how strong your mother was, but I didn't tell you that I also saw her cry sometimes," Darcy said.

Melinda narrowed her eyes at Darcy and then turned her head away. She couldn't remember ever seeing her mother cry.

"It's true, Mel," Darcy continued. "The first day home from the hospital, she sat on the couch in the living room and bawled her eyes out. Not because of you. You were her pride and joy from that day on. I think she was lonely for the people back home."

Melinda shuffled her shoe across the carpet and bit her lip.

"I'm telling you this so you know that it's okay to feel sad. You are going to miss home and your mom and maybe even me," Darcy said trying to hold back the tears. "I know I'm going to miss you." She wiped her wet cheeks with her sleeve. "You are going to meet some new people, make some new friends and see a whole other world from little old Shorewood Beach. Think of it as an adventure."

The overhead speaker blared, "Final boarding call for flight 1513 to Chicago."

A flight attendant stood near Melinda waiting to escort her to the airplane.

Melinda and Darcy hugged. Darcy shook in Melinda's arms.

Darcy pulled back and attempted a smile. She pulled a plastic bag from her purse and handed it to Melinda. "Sorry I didn't have time to wrap this."

Melinda reached in and found a package of stationery with a picture of Sally's Rock on it.

"It's for you to write me," Darcy said. "I put some stamps in there too, and I wrote my address on all the envelopes."

"Good luck, Mel. Call me anytime. Take care of yourself."

Darcy burst into tears, and Melinda hugged her. "It's okay Darc. I'll be okay. Don't worry about me." She then turned and followed the woman in the blue uniform down the jetway.

Chapter 3

The exhaustion of the past week's activities and the lull of the jet engines put Melinda to sleep soon after take off. She didn't wake until the overhead lights turned on and the flight attendant welcomed them to O'Hare International Airport in Chicago.

Melinda waited for everyone else to exit the plane before the flight attendant met her to walk her to the gate. She felt embarrassed to have to be chaperoned on and off the plane.

As they neared the waiting crowd, Melinda's heart thumped beneath her blue sweater, the one that kept her warm at the football game on that fateful night. She hadn't had much time to think about meeting her uncle, but now with each step she became more anxious. Would he recognize her? Would he be nice? How should she greet him? Should she give him a hug or just shake his hand? Would he look like her mother? She'd seen only one picture of him when he was a kid. He was in his 40s now. Maybe he wouldn't even be here. Maybe he would send her to an orphanage in a slum of Chicago. She'd read about orphanages in big cities. People only adopted the babies. The older kids had to help cook and clean. Her palms were sweating and she wiped them on her jeans.

The flight attendant led her into the gate area. Just a few people were still standing around talking. Melinda scanned the crowd, but didn't see a man who looked like he was waiting for her.

She followed the flight attendant to the counter where she asked another woman in uniform if anyone had inquired about Melinda. The woman shook her head and looked back down at the computer screen. The flight attendant frowned.

"Well, let me see what I'm going to do with you until we get this figured out. . ."

Just then someone yelled, "I'm here. I'm here."

Melinda turned to see a short black woman hurrying through the crowd in the large airport hallway. The woman smiled at Melinda.

"Oh my gawd child, you look just like your mother. If I didn't know better, I'd think I just went back 15 years and this was Carole looking back at me. I knew it was you from clear over there. Turn around and let me see you," she said. The woman touched Melinda's shoulder and helped her turn in a circle.

"There are a few differences. Your hair is darker and not as wavy. Your eyes are greener. Your face is a little longer and skinnier. Little bigger nose and a clef in the chin. But you have the same body, long and so strong. The same beautiful baby soft skin. Where are all the zits kids your age are supposed to get? You lucky dog you."

Melinda stared speechless at this woman who seemed to know so much about her mother. She must have been just 5' tall. She had silver-gray hair that was pulled on top of her head. Her glasses sat low on her nose and she tilted her head up to look at Melinda. Her oversized shiny purple and white jacket sleeves were so long that her fingertips barely showed.

"Where are my manners?" She chuckled to herself. "My name is Gloria Behn. I work for your Uncle Charles. He wasn't able to pick you up so he asked me to do it."

"Glory B." The words escaped Melinda's mouth before she realized she said them out loud. She knew the name.

"That's right child. Gloria, Glory or Glory B. Whatever you want to call me. You can call me one or all of them. You may even come up with something else you want to call me. Ha. Lord knows I've been called all sorts of things. Your mother talked about me, did she? Well, you don't believe everything you hear, do ya?"

She reached over and held Melinda's forearm as she laughed.

"My mama and daddy, bless their souls, named me Gloria centuries ago. My brothers and sisters started calling me Glory when I was a baby. And then when's I got older and started getting myself into troubles, my mamma started calling me Glory B. She'd yell 'Glory B.

Child what are you up to now?' Guess you can figure out how that name stuck so good."

Glory laughed again. Melinda couldn't help but smile too.

"Look at you. Turn around." Glory turned Melinda all the way around again. "You really are the spittin' image of her. No one could argue that. No, not one single person who knows you both. Let me see if you have that dimple in the right cheek. Grin a little, honey. Oh, lordy, you do. Isn't that great. Come here child. I need a hug. I need to hug my little Carole's baby."

Glory grabbed Melinda and pulled her into her arms. She seemed unusually strong for her size and age. She squeezed Melinda hard like she was never going to let go. In her ear, she whispered.

"I'm so sorry about your mamma. So sorry honey. I loved her like one of my own. I was so sad when she just up and left. Didn't tell anyone. Didn't even tell me she was pregnant. I gave her a hard time about that at first, but a person's gotta do what a person's gotta do."

Gloria patted Melinda's cheek.

"She did a right good job raising you it looks like to me."

Melinda looked back into the brownest eyes she'd ever seen. Gloria glanced up at a nearby airport screen.

"Listen to me just babbling on when we should be going to find your bags. I talk more when I'm excited, and I'm excited to see you. Looky here. This will tell us where to pick up your bags. Baggage claim 7. Well, where the heck is that? They don't tell us that."

Glory looked left, then right.

"Well, let's see. I get so turned around in this airport. I think it is the biggest one in the world. Or was it the busiest? Oh wait, I see a sign for the baggage claim areas."

Glory laughed. "Once, Fred saw a sign like that very one and that old fart grabbed me and hugged me in front of a bunch of people and said, 'Here, I claim my baggage right here.' Believe me, I gave him a big wallop across the shoulder. He said, 'Honey, I meant it in a good way. You know, like a treasure.' He loved to tease me. Oh, I wish you could have met him. He loved your mama too. He used to kid her and tell her that her hair was turning red, redder than a rose. He died last year. Bless his soul."

"I'm sorry," Melinda said. When she said it, she realized that she really was sorry that this kind-hearted woman, whom she'd just met, had lost her husband.

"Thank you, honey," Glory said. "I get sad from time to time and miss him so bad it hurts all over. But then I remember what a joy he was in my life and I get happy that I was lucky enough to have him as part of my life. You know, I feel like he's still here sometimes. I even talk to him and feel like he answers me back. I don't know. Maybe it's because I knew him so well that I know what he would answer if he were here. Like right now, he'd probably tell me I'm talking too much and that I should just hush up. And he'd say that I talk a bunch whether I'm excited or not. 'Tell the girl the truth Glory,' he'd say."

They walked quietly for a while.

"You work for my uncle?" Melinda said.

"Yes, I am Jacob and Samuel's nanny, like I was your mamma's and Charles' nanny. And I clean your uncle's house, do his laundry, buy his groceries and whatever else he might ask me to do, just as I did with Mr. and Mrs. Overstreet for all those years. Jacob and Samuel live with their mother now though, after the divorce and all. So I watch them at her house when they're there and at your uncle's house sometimes when they're there. You haven't met the twins yet, have you?"

Melinda shook her head.

"Just starting kindergarten this year. Jacob talks a little more than Samuel, but they're both full of energy. They're pretty good boys really."

"I haven't met my uncle yet either," Melinda said.

"That's right you haven't," Glory said. "Oh, he's a character. I started being a nanny when your mamma was just a baby and Charles was about eight. They had the same parents and I brought 'em up the same, but they were never anything alike. Kids from the same family can be so different. Charles, he likes to compete, and win. Your mama, she didn't have a competitive streak in her, except in running. She wanted to be on the cross-country team at school so bad, but your grandmother wouldn't let her. Wasn't lady-like enough for Mrs. Overstreet's tastes. Your mama was born to run." Glory glanced at Melinda. "Whew. Could that girl run like the wind!"

"I like to run too," Melinda said. "It was one of our favorite things to do together."

"Good for you," said Glory. "Well, Charles is a big time downtown lawyer. Runs your grandfather's old firm. Sometimes, I think Charles doesn't know how to care . . .

Well, look at me getting ready to be nasty or something. I know you'll be fine with your uncle. If he doesn't treat you nice, I'll keep him in line. If Charles or anyone else ever bothers you, you just let Glory B. know. I'll take care of it. We're going to be right close, you and me. We are. Okay?" Glory put her arm around Melinda's shoulder.

"Okay," Melinda said with a grin as they came upon the baggage claim area.

They found Melinda's two duffle bags Darcy bought at Fred's Thrift Shop, and they walked outside across three lanes of traffic. Doors popped open and slammed shut. People jumped in and out of backseats. Cars stopped. Cars roared away. Darcy was right. There *were* a lot of taxis in Chicago.

The lights in the parking lot made it as bright as day. Just like in the airport, Melinda was surprised at how many people were out this late at night. At home, when it got dark, the town quieted down to a peaceful hush. She loved to walk on the beach with her mom and point out different star constellations. As they exited the garage, she looked up, but couldn't see a single star, only tall buildings with reflective walls.

They pulled onto the highway. Cars sped along bumper to bumper, dodging, swerving, honking.

"I've never seen so many cars," Melinda said, "especially at night. Is something going on, a festival or big meeting?"

Glory chuckled. "Chicago's always like this, day or night. This is nothing really. We're cruising now. Wait until you see it during the day. You could be totally stopped in traffic for an hour."

"This is nothing like Shorewood," Melinda said. "We walked everywhere. Of course, we didn't even have a car since mom didn't drive."

"Didn't drive?"

"Never."

"Oh, she used to drive. Took her to driver's training myself, " Glory said. "I bet she stopped driving 'cause of that accident."

"What accident?"

"The one she had right before she left. It was a tragic one, but not her fault like some said."

Melinda couldn't believe her ears. She was too embarrassed to tell Glory that her mother had never mentioned a "tragic" accident. She thought her mom said she had never gotten her license, ever. Why would she have said that?

"You've had a long day, and night," Glory said. "We have at least a 30 minute drive. Just close your eyes and rest. If you fall asleep, I'll wake you up when we get there."

"I slept on the plane. I'm not tired now," Melinda said. "Is my uncle waiting for us at his house?"

"No, your uncle and the boys went to Australia. They'll be back Sunday night. I get to have you all to myself for a couple days. We're going to my house now."

Melinda felt relieved. Staying at Glory's sounded better than going to her uncle's.

"Is that why my uncle didn't come to Oregon last week? Because he was in Australia?"

Gloria looked quickly across the seat at Melinda.

"Oh, yes honey," she said. "I guess no one told you. I was watching Charles' house while he was gone. I checked the messages for him. He said he didn't want to be bothered unless it was real important. So when I heard the message from your mom's friend."

"Darcy," Melinda interrupted.

"When I heard the message from Darcy, I called Charles right away. He wasn't in the room, so I left a message with the hotel. They had to track him down. He was on a tour in the Outback for a couple days and was hard to get a hold of. When he finally called me back, it was the day before the funeral. There's a big time difference between here and Australia, twelve hours or something. He said there was no way he could make it in time. He asked me to send some really nice flowers. Did you see the flowers from your uncle?"

Melinda nodded.

They turned off the highway onto a crowded street with lots of fast food restaurants, a McDonald's every six blocks it seemed. After going through several stoplights, they turned onto a small rutted road that led into a large apartment complex.

"I'm sorry your uncle wasn't there," Glory said. "I gave him my opinion, but he said I didn't know nothing about international travel, and that it was foolish to hold off on the funeral due to him."

"I don't care if he was there," Melinda said. "I don't even know him."

"Did your mama talk about him?"

"Some. Mostly family memories. Vacations and stuff like that. She said he was a lot older. When I was little

I asked lots of questions about where my dad was, why my grandparents didn't come see me and things like that. Mom never said much and I quit asking." Melinda was curious about Charles, but even more, she wondered about her dad, the person no one ever mentioned. She thought about asking Glory now. The woman sitting next to her probably had all the answers, but Melinda didn't know if she was ready for them yet.

Glory parked along the small street in front of one of the buildings.

As they approached a green door with the number 6 on it, Glory said, "Fred and me got lucky when we found this place. We wanted an apartment on the first floor and this one was open. I didn't want to pack groceries up stairs anymore. We got our own little yard too, instead of just a tiny balcony like those up there. It gave the kids a little room to run around when they were little, and a place for me and Fred to sit sometimes. We paid extra to have 'em build the fence for some privacy."

Glory unlocked the door, turned on the light and hung her coat on a rack near the entrance.

"It's humble, but it's home," she said as she walked toward the kitchen. "Come on in. Make yourself comfortable."

Melinda dropped her bags by the front door and glanced around the room. She'd never seen so much stuff in one house. Every space was filled. She didn't know where to look first. A large flowered sofa, the biggest thing in the room, was against the far wall. Pillows of all shapes and sizes completely covered it. A worn brown recliner made of cracked plastic had a blanket folded over it and next to that was a small TV stand. Family photographs, cross-stitched prayers, scenery pictures and a big black and white picture of Jesus covered the walls. A glass cabinet with little ceramic figures was next to the front door. Guidepost magazines and TV Guides were scattered on tables and chairs.

Melinda followed Glory through the arched entry into the kitchen. A small microwave sat on a TV stand near the door. A trashcan was squeezed in between it and the corner. The counter was full of cereal boxes, round silver canisters labeled "Sugar," "Flour," "Coffee," and "Tea," and a blue plastic holder stacked with clean dishes. The kitchen table, covered with a thin green tablecloth, was almost too big for the space it was allotted in the corner. Glory placed her big black purse on the table and tried to cover up a yawn.

"Oh, excuse me," she said. "All of the sudden I'm so tired. Let's get ready for bed. Follow me and I'll show you your room." They walked down a short hallway lined with framed photographs. "This is the bathroom. This is your room and this is mine. Small and cozy, uh?"

"I like it. It's about the same size as our house."

They entered a room at the end of the hall.

"I pulled the sofa bed out and got it all ready for you. My grandkids play in here a lot plus it's my storage room too so it's kind of cramped. I'll leave a washrag and towel out for you in the bathroom. Do you need anything else?"

Melinda shook her head. Glory gave her a hug and walked out. Melinda looked around the room and then sat down on the bed and let her head fall forward. She felt tired now, but more than that, an overwhelming sadness came over her. This was her first night away from home. She wondered if she would ever see Oregon again. She was glad Glory was in the bathroom because tears were starting to slip from her eyes. She missed her house, her room, Darcy and most of all, her mother.

She tried to think about something good, about how nice Glory was. She sniffled as Glory walked near her door.

"Are you okay honey?" Glory asked standing in the entryway.

Melinda ran her fingers through her hair and shook her head. Glory sat on the bed next to her and cradled her head.

"I can't help it." Melinda began. "I'm trying not to."

"It's okay sweetie," Glory interrupted. "It's okay."

Melinda reached her arms around Glory and all the tears she'd suppressed for the past week fell. The two sat on the bed embracing. Glory gently rocked Melinda as she trembled and cried harder. She rubbed the back of Melinda's head and kept repeating, "Sweet child of God. Oh Lord, have mercy on this sweet child of God."

To Melinda, she said, "Tomorrow will be a brighter day." Melinda doubted it, but she hoped that Glory was right.

Chapter 4

The next morning Melinda woke up in the unfamiliar room. Sunlight seeped through the edges of the pulled blind. Melinda lay on her back looking around as the items surrounding her slowly came into focus. It took her a minute to remember she'd been brought here by Glory B. Melinda had never met anyone like Glory B. Chicago wasn't nearly as forbidding as she had expected. She had a friend.

She pulled the covers back, eased up and then squeezed in the narrow space between the bed and the bookcase. Just as she opened the door, Glory appeared.

"There you are, sleepy head," Glory said. "I was starting to think you were going to sleep the entire day. Follow me. I have some people who can't wait to meet you. Cute PJs." Glory took Melinda's hand and led her down the hall. Melinda squinted, then rubbed her eyes, trying to help adjust to the bright lights. She glanced down at her pink and blue pajamas covered with white tumbling teddy bears. She couldn't remember changing into them last night.

Now, she felt Glory's warm hand wrapped around hers as they moved together toward the smell of bacon and coffee and the sound of laughter. Next to her new companion, she walked lighter than she had in days.

"It's nearly lunchtime," Glory continued. "Sleep. Sleep. Sleep. That's a teenager for you. I've been around enough of them in my life. You know I have a granddaughter about your age. You'll meet her. She's something else."

Glory stopped talking as they passed the small kitchen nook and stood in front of the table that was an array of newspapers and coffee cups.

"Melinda, I want you to meet some of my family," Glory said. She placed her arm around Melinda's shoulder and pulled her close. "Let me warn you. They're a little crazy in the head. This here's my big brother Leroy." A large man wearing a Chicago Cub's baseball cap nodded and tilted his coffee cup toward Melinda. She felt self-conscious in her pajamas and tried to stand behind a chair.

"Now, little sister you know what I said about calling me your BIG brother," Leroy said. "You promised me you wouldn't say BIG anymore. You forgot already." A couple of people at the table snickered. Melinda thought about asking Glory if it would be okay for her to go change clothes.

"Excuuuuse me," Glory said to the ceiling. "I mean my OLDER brother Leroy. Is that better? Don't pay no attention to him, Melinda. He's big and he's old and he knows it." Glory stuck out her tongue at Leroy. "These are my *nice* relatives, my sister Faith and niece Talisha."

The two women smiled at Melinda, and Faith said, "Hi, sweetie. So sorry about your mother," sounding almost just like Glory. Faith looked like Glory too, only slightly thinner and taller. Talisha nodded in agreement to her mother's sentiment.

Glory pointed to a pretty woman at the end of the table. "And this sweet young thing is my daughter Brandy Lee. She was one of your mama's best friends."

Brandy Lee smiled at Melinda. Her eyes had a sparkle to them. Her full red lips parted revealing straight white teeth. "Nice to meet you Melinda. I'm so sorry to hear about your mama. She was a dear friend."

Melinda tried to remember her mother's childhood stories and the name Brandy Lee, but the stories were so long ago and so few, Melinda's memory failed her. Did her mom ever mention a friend at all?

"Wait, I heard some words to correct again, Glory B.," Leroy yelled. "You said SWEET and YOUNG to describe someone." He rolled his eyes toward Brandy Lee, who quickly furrowed her brow and scrunched her lips toward him. "Uncle Leroy!"

Everyone laughed including Brandy Lee. Glory's hearty laugh was the loudest of all. Melinda looked sideways at the woman now so near to her. She had a mole just above her lip and another one on her lift cheek. Her skin was dark and smooth with laugh lines around her eyes and mouth. When she smiled and laughed, her eyes all but disappeared. Her black hair was coarse and perfectly in place.

Glory's eyes met Melinda's and she tightened her grip on Melinda's shoulder. "Let's get you something to eat. I made biscuits and gravy and bacon for breakfast, but you slept right through it and then *someone* ate it all." She tilted her head toward the crew at the table peering directly at Leroy whose round belly rose above the table.

"Sister, I heard that!"

Glory handed Melinda several things from the refrigerator. They looked like lunch items. Her mother had always stressed the importance of starting the day with a good breakfast. She didn't know whether to say anything or just be happy to have something to eat at all. She realized that her appetite was starting to come back.

"Round two," Glory said. "We'll fill the table back up with food again."

"Let me help you, mama," Brandy Lee said, walking into the small kitchen.

The two women pulled food from everywhere. From the refrigerator, salad, coleslaw, lunchmeat, mustard and mayonnaise appeared. From the cabinets, they brought out pickles, chips and crackers.

Melinda took a seat between Glory and Brandy Lee and watched as arms stretched across the table in all directions. Melinda was hungry. After hesitating for a few minutes, she made a plate for herself.

Two conversations were going on at the same time, one at each end of the table. Melinda heard Talisha tell a funny story about a woman forgetting to put her skirt on over her slip before coming to work. Leroy said he could top that and told about a man who came to the steel mill in his house slippers and boxer shorts. Melinda caught herself giggling. Just yesterday, she hadn't thought that was possible ever again. She covered her mouth with her hand and looked down at her plate, but the snickers kept coming. When she looked up, all eyes were on her. Glory smiled.

"That's good sweetie. Laughter is good," Glory said. "You know, it reminds me of your mama. She loved to laugh."

"Glory B.," Faith said. "Remember when Carole used to count how many times you laughed in one day? What was your record? Fifty, 100?"

"Two," Leroy interrupted.

Melinda joined the laughter easily this time. She took another bite of her sandwich and glanced around the table at all the smiling faces, feeling like she'd always known these people.

"Don't you laugh at his jokes too," Glory said, pointing at Melinda. "I'm already outnumbered. Okay, if we all stop laughing at his bad jokes, maybe he'll go away." Glory stood up and began clearing the table. She patted Melinda on the shoulder as she walked by. "Your mama used to love eating sandwiches for breakfast."

The front door flew open and a girl about Melinda's age bounded across the room to the table. She bent down and kissed Brandy Lee on the cheek.

"Hey, Mom. Hey, everybody," she said. "What's to eat? I'm starved."

Brandy Lee fanned her arm across the table. "What you see is what you get. We've all been helping ourselves as usual, dear. How was your run?"

"I decided I hate cross country," the girl said.

"Why do you do it then?" Faith asked.

"It helps my sprints."

The girl looked around the entire table and suddenly noticed Melinda.

"Melinda, this is my daughter Jillian," Brandy Lee said. "She just went for a long run."

"Really long. Too long," Jillian said.

"She's a sprinter, but track season's in the spring. It's just cross country right now."

"But Mom remember, we have two big invitational meets that are both track and cross country. One is in the fall and one in the spring. So everyone needs to practice all year. The long distance is supposed to help sprinters too, but I don't know."

Glory stood in the doorway. "I didn't get a hug, baby."

Jillian hugged Glory then she took a seat opposite Melinda.

"You know your mama was a great long distance runner," Brandy Lee said looking at Melinda. "She used to love it more than anything when she was younger."

"She still loved it," Melinda said. "We ran together all the time."

"Grams said you are starting at Roosevelt on Monday and will be in eighth grade too," Jillian said. "Wanna go out for the cross country team with me? We could use a good long distance runner."

"I don't know," Melinda said. "I've never been on a team. I just ran with my mom."

Jillian stuffed a big bite of her sandwich in her mouth, chewed for several seconds and then, in between swallows, said, "You'll be looking for ways to escape that house and get away from Charles."

"Jillian," Brandy Lee scolded. "That isn't nice, and Melinda hasn't even met her Uncle Charles yet."

Still with her head down over her sandwich that was now leaking mayonnaise and mustard onto her plate, Jillian mumbled, "You're not missing much."

"Jillian. Stop. If you can't say anything nice, be quiet."

Jillian rolled her eyes. She looked across the table at Melinda. "Cute PJs." Her mother looked at her sternly. "Really, mom. I'm being serious. I have some almost just like them, but they have bunnies instead of bears. Remember?" She raised her eyebrows at her mother.

Melinda looked down and realized she was the only one still in her pajamas. It was after one o'clock. She stood up, "Nice to meet you," she said to Jillian, then carried her plate into the kitchen where Glory was doing dishes.

"I told you she was something," Glory said. "But very likable once you get to know her." After finishing a big stack of dishes, Melinda asked if she could take a shower.

She emerged from the bathroom several minutes later feeling much more comfortable in her faded jeans and t-shirt. She tied the blue sweater around her waist, and pulled her thick, wavy hair back into a ponytail.

As she walked down the hall, Melinda heard Glory say, "I don't know how much she knows. She didn't even know Carole ever drove a car."

Melinda entered the living room where Glory, Brandy Lee and Jillian were sitting.

"Everyone else had to leave, but said they'd see you again soon," Glory said. "This is Maybelle. She's a friend from way back." Melinda hadn't noticed the small woman in the corner who had a coffee cup covering the bottom half of her face. Over the next several hours, the house was a constant stream of people. Melinda was amazed at the number of family members, friends and neighbors visiting all in one day just like they did it every day of the year. Most of the time, she sat quietly listening. Everyone acknowledged her and expressed their sympathy for her recent loss.

Melinda watched Jillian sit next to her mother and flip through magazines and catalogs until Glory or Brandy Lee asked her to get a guest a cup of coffee, tea or water. Jillian had big brown eyes with long lashes. Although she was pretty like her mother, Melinda noticed many differences. Jillian's nose was thinner. Her lips were full, but not nearly as much as her mother's. Her skin was paler and her hair, pulled back in a ponytail like Melinda's, was thinner and much lighter, not black like the others.

As Glory stood with the door open and the last guests took their leave, Jillian and Melinda carried glasses into the kitchen.

"Do you want to run with me tomorrow?" Jillian asked. "I could meet you here after church."

Melinda placed two glasses in the sink. She missed running and the feeling it gave her, but it seemed so soon after her mother's death. She had never run without her mom.

"I don't know," she said.

"I'll tell you what," Jillian said. "You don't have to decide now. I'll stop by tomorrow. If you want to, great. If you don't, that's okay too. See you tomorrow."

• • •

That night before Melinda went to sleep, Glory stopped by her room. "How are you doing, sweetie?"

"I'm fine. Thanks for everything."

Glory sat down on the edge of the bed. "You seem a little sad. Is everything okay?"

Melinda took a deep breath. "Jillian asked me to run with her tomorrow."

"That's great."

"I don't know if I want to."

"But, you said you love to run just like your mamma and it was your favorite thing to do together."

"That's it. She's not here anymore. I don't know if I want to run anymore, or if I even can without her."

"Sweet, sweet child," Glory said, placing her hand on Melinda's cheek. "Of course you can. You won't be running without her. She's always with you. She lives on in you child. Can't you see it? Can't you feel it?"

Melinda thought about Glory's words. She wanted them to be true, but she shook her head. Glory smiled.

"You will sweetheart. As long as you are alive, your mother lives through you. If she loved to run, you should do it for her, for that part of her that lives on in you."

Chapter 5

When Melinda awoke the next day, she rummaged through her backpack and pulled out the stationary Darcy had given her at the airport.

Dear Darcy,

Can't believe I've only been away one full day. It seems like so long ago that I left home and you. I haven't even met my uncle. I'm glad about that. I'm at Glory B's. She was the one mom always said raised her. She feels like a grandmother I never knew. She has a daughter that was good friends with mom, and a granddaughter my age who asked me to go running with her today. I feel a little guilty about running without mom. You know I've already learned lots of things about mom that I didn't know. Did you know she used to have a driver's license? She used to drive! I know this is a strange question at this point in time, but why don't I know anything about my dad? Do you know anything about him?

I'm just thinking maybe he would be better to live with than my uncle. I haven't heard anything good about Charles. Hope all is well at The Loft and that you get your car paid off soon so you can come visit me. I miss you.

   Love,
   Mel

Jillian arrived after church as she said. She wore a Roosevelt school t-shirt and blue shorts with a white stripe down each side. Melinda watched Jillian grab a corner of the couch with one hand and her worn tennis shoe with the other, stretching her leg back behind her.

"Ready to go?" Jillian said.

Melinda nodded, took off her blue sweater and placed it gently on the back of a chair near the door so she'd know right where it was when she got back.

"How long do you want to go?" Jillian said walking out the door.

Melinda shrugged and followed. She wondered how they were going to run through the busy streets.

"I need to go at least 30 minutes today," Jillian said. "Is that cool with you? Okay. Stick close. Traffic is a drag, but I've learned how to dash and dodge at just the right time. If you get tired just let me know. We can stop and rest anytime you want. Cool? Cool."

Melinda got in step with Jillian as they jogged away from the apartment complex. She kept her eyes on the unfamiliar sidewalks, but also tried to see everything they passed. Row after row of small brick houses were on their right, while parked cars lined the street on their left. Dogs barked from behind chain-link fences, men in slippers retrieved newspapers from their front porches and an occasional church door opened revealing lots of women in silky, flowered dresses emerging onto the lawns.

They rounded a corner and emerged onto a busy street with gas stations, hair salons, Burger Kings, Taco Bells and small shopping plazas with pawn shops, butcher shops and movie rental stores.

"I live down that way a little bit." Jillian pointed to a street to their left. "And Roosevelt is that way." She pointed to the right. Jillian was breathing hard and her words came out between breaths.

"Do you need a break?" Jillian shouted to Melinda.

"No, I'm okay." Melinda said. "Do you think we could run past the school?"

"Sure."

They ran three more blocks before Jillian stopped in front of a two-story, brick building with the name "Roosevelt Middle School" engraved in stone blocks above a series of glass doors. Jillian bent over, her back heaving up and down.

"I don't know about you, but that was a good workout for me," Jillian said.

Melinda had never seen such a big school just for sixth, seventh and eighth graders. They walked around the side and Melinda's eyes followed the brick wall the length of the block. As they continued, she saw the fenced-in track and bleachers.

Jillian stopped at the fence. "That's where all my dreams get squashed."

Melinda looked at Jillian confused.

"I just want to be good at something. I thought maybe it would be track," Jillian said. "In grade school,

I did great in sprints. But so many kids from so many different elementary schools go to school here, and now I'm just okay. I've never even received a ribbon at a meet since I started middle school."

Melinda looked back toward the school. "This is huge," she said. "My school wasn't even half this big and it had kindergarteners to eighth graders in it."

"Why didn't you do track or cross country? Was your school too small?"

"No, we had sports teams and track. We competed against other small schools like us. I just liked running with Mom I guess. It was kind of our special thing."

Jillian walked onto the field. "Maybe I'll practice a few sprints. Wanna do some with me?"

"No way."

"That's right. You're a distance runner, not a sprinter."

Melinda laughed. "I don't think I'm either really."

"Are you kidding? We just ran about two miles and you weren't even winded at all. You looked like you were going for a walk in the park. One more minute and I would have probably passed out."

Jillian stood on the asphalt track and stretched forward with one leg extended in front and the other bent behind her. Melinda sat on the grass near a stack of hurdles. She watched Jillian bend down low and then dash as fast as she could three quarters of the length of the straight-away. After repeating the pattern back and forth several times, Jillian plopped down next to Melinda and fell back looking up at the sky.

"See, I stink."

"You look fast to me. Your legs are so strong. I can't imagine anyone beating you."

"You'll see. They're all faster. And I'm sick of it."

Melinda propped her feet on a metal hurdle. "Ever tried these?"

Jillian lifted her head slightly to see. "No," she said, then let it fall back down to the ground. She suddenly jumped up in one giant leap.

"Why didn't I ever think of that before? Melinda, you're a genius."

Jillian started pulling the hurdles apart and dragging them onto the track. "Why didn't I ever think of this?" She repeated the question several times. "I was so set on winning the 50 yard or 100 yard dash, I didn't even think of doing anything else. You know, I've jumped the bushes in our front yard since I was a baby. Well, maybe not quite that long ago." Jillian spread three hurdles a few yards apart along the track. "Do you know how far these should be apart?

"You're asking me?" Melinda said.

"Yeah, right. Why would you know? Have you ever even seen a track meet?"

Melinda shook her head, and then blurted, "Wait. I've watched the Olympics."

"Well, girl you're going to one in person now. You are going to be my biggest hurdles fan. You were the one who turned me on to this. There. That looks about right." After moving the hurdles a few feet further apart, Jillian stood back with her hands on her hips examining them.

"Don't you think you should wait until practice to try this?" Melinda said. "What if you fall and kill yourself?"

"Have you ever heard of someone killing themselves on the hurdles? No. Just chill out and watch this. And don't worry. Our bushes are taller and wider."

"Wait," Melinda screamed just as Jillian started to run.

She skidded to a stop. "What?"

"That one's turned different than the others."

Jillian laughed and jogged over to turn the hurdle completely around. "Thanks," she yelled. "Okay, here goes nothing."

Melinda was afraid to watch. She covered her eyes with her hand, but parted her fingers so she could see as Jillian bent to her ready position, then dashed toward the first hurdle. *Jump*, Melinda thought. Jillian's foot hit the first hurdle, but she kept running. Her right leg flew through the air and totally cleared the second hurdle and the third hurdle.

"Yes!" she screamed and raised her arms into the air. "I can do it. You're right, I better wait until practice tomorrow."

Melinda started laughing. "I meant before you tried it at all."

Jillian danced around in a circle waving her arms high in the air.

"Melinda, you made my day and maybe my whole career. I'll be thanking you when I get that college scholarship and when I win that Gold Medal. Come on, let's go have a sundae. On me. Well, it'll be on my dad. He's the manager at Dairy Queen. And, by the way, you have to be on the team. You are my good luck charm."

Chapter 6

At Dairy Queen, Melinda scanned the workers behind the counter trying to pick out Jillian's father. Her friends' dads always intrigued her, the way they talked to their daughters, the way they paid attention or didn't pay attention to the girls' chatter. A young black man helped a customer and another stuffed a bag with French fries. They looked too young. A man as white as Melinda turned around near the shake machine, placed a lid on the cup and smiled up at Jillian.

"That's your dad?" Melinda didn't mean to sound so surprised, but he wasn't at all what she was expecting. She'd never known anyone with one black parent and one white.

Jillian laughed. "Yes." He walked through a door and to the other side of the counter next to the girls. "Dad, this is my new friend, Melinda. She's going to be on the track team with me, and she's an awesome cross country runner, and she just had the most brilliant idea."

Jillian's dad seemed to never stop smiling. He motioned for the three of them to sit at a table in the corner. To one of the teenagers behind the counter, he yelled, "Anthony, can you bring us three peanut butter parfaits? Is that all right with you Melinda?" Melinda nodded.

"Coming right up, Mr. Jones."

Mr. Jones was tall with thinning blond hair that came to a point in the middle of his forehead. Jillian's unique features that Melinda had noticed at Glory's became even more apparent as she compared the two at the table. Jillian had her father's eyes, deep set, round and hazel green. She was sure she remembered Glory's and Brandy Lee's being almost black. Jillian's hair wasn't as light as her father's or nearly as dark as her mother's, but a medium brown somewhere in between her parents. Melinda thought the unique combination of dark skin, light hair and green eyes was fitting for Jillian.

As the three ate their ice cream, Jillian talked about doing the hurdles and how it was all Melinda's idea. Mr. Jones stared at his daughter, glanced at Melinda now and then, and listened to every word like it was the most important thing he'd ever heard. Men intrigued Melinda, and on the rare occasion when she spent time with them, she found herself closely observing their behavior.

"Oh, Dad, wait 'til you see. I float over those hurdles just like I do the bushes in our yard. I can win this event. I'm really good at it. You should see me."

"A little dramatic at times," Mr. Jones said, shifting his smile from Jillian to Melinda for a moment.

"Just be careful," he said to Jillian. "I've seen the results of you not making it over the bushes."

Jillian started laughing, nearly choking on her ice cream. She tried to talk, but held up one finger while she swallowed the big spoonful in her mouth.

"Melinda stopped me from jumping over a hurdle that was backwards," Jillian said. "That would have been a bad hurdle to not make it over. I wouldn't be so happy right now if I had missed that one. I could see the school paper headlines now. Jumping Jones hurdles to the ground on first attempt to make hurdle team."

Jillian laughed so hard, Melinda and Mr. Jones couldn't help but join her.

"Just like your grandmother always says, 'You're something else Jillian Jones.'" Mr. Jones stood up. "Nice to meet you, Melinda. I better get back to work. See you at home in a couple hours, honey." He bent down and kissed Jillian on the top of her head.

The girls watched Mr. Jones walk back behind the counter. He greeted the customers and employees with a smile, and Melinda decided she liked him a lot.

Melinda looked at her new friend across the table. She was thankful to have met Jillian so quickly, but an overwhelming sadness came over her and she suddenly wished she was alone in her mother's room again.

"What's wrong?" Jillian said softly.

Melinda forced a smile. "I don't know."

"Did I say something wrong? Did my dad?"

"No. You're great. Your parents are great. You're lucky."

"Yeah, I guess I am. My parents are cool."

Melinda watched the traffic out the window. Cars were backed up at the stoplight and a woman pushed a stroller through the intersection to the other side.

"Miss your mom?" Jillian said.

Melinda nodded. In the parking lot, a man opened the car door for his wife while two kids scrambled out of the backseat.

"What about your dad?"

Melinda shrugged. "I don't know anything about him. Never met him."

"Did your mom talk about him?"

"Never. And I never even cared." She swirled the vanilla ice cream with the chocolate sauce until it was totally brown. "Until now."

Melinda started to talk, stopped, then said, "I haven't told anyone, but I'm curious now. While you were talking to your dad, I thought about how my own dad could live right here. My mom must have met him around here. She was pregnant when she moved to Oregon. He could be that guy right there." She pointed to the man walking in with the woman and two kids.

"I could help you find him." Jillian's eyes grew wider. "We could find him. Maybe he'd be this really nice guy and you'd have this spectacular reunion. I've seen it happen on TV. Then you wouldn't have to live with your Uncle Charles."

"What is my uncle like?"

"I haven't heard him talk much. He always has his head up in the air like everyone else is below him," Jillian replied. "He looks like one of those stuffed shirt lawyers that keep hounding at the guy on the stand until the guy breaks down and cries. Then he turns around with a smirk on his face and sits back down in his chair. I can't imagine living with him."

"Thanks," Melinda said. "You're making me feel a lot better."

"Don't worry about Charles," Jillian said. "You won't have to live with him long. We'll find your dad. We could start by asking my mom and Grams. They knew your mom before she moved."

"Have you ever heard them say anything about it?"

"No."

"I don't know. I don't want to make it a big deal," Melinda said. "What if we find out something really bad, or what if he's worse than Charles? If he was so great, why didn't my mom stay with him?"

"Don't worry."

"You're always saying 'don't worry.' Have you noticed that?"

"I can be very sneaky. No one will even suspect anything. If we find out something bad, we just stop there. No harm done," Jillian said. "You helped me, now I'll help you. Oh, man." Jillian suddenly looked angry. Melinda followed her gaze out the window to a group of girls walking toward Dairy Queen.

"These are not the type of girls you'll meet at Roosevelt," Jillian said. "I'm telling you that right now. They may be the type you'll meet in your new neighborhood though. I can't stand them. They go to Trinity. It's a private school you should feel lucky you're not going to. Your uncle went there. Your mom went there. Your ancestors started it or something. They think they are better than everyone else just because they wear fancy clothes, their daddies drive Mercedes and Jaguars and their mamas spend all their time at the country club."

Three girls walked in and stood at the counter. Mr. Jones said, "Hello, girls. How are you today?" It was the first time Melinda saw him not smiling.

The girls didn't smile either or even answer his question. The girl in the front had blond hair that almost looked white. She said, "I'll have a Diet Coke."

"That's it?" Mr. Jones said.

The blond girl nodded and the two behind her said they'd have the same. They each had on a plaid skirt and matching sweater, patent-leather shoes and headbands in their perfectly trimmed hair.

The blond girl locked eyes with Jillian before sitting at a table near them. The girl made it obvious that she was looking at Jillian's worn tennis shoes and faded gray shorts.

"I almost forgot that track season starts next week. I haven't practiced all summer. Have you?" Blondie said to her friends who shook their heads and sipped from their straws. "But, some of us don't have to practice to win." The girls chuckled.

Jillian winked at Melinda. "Melinda, thanks for the great run this morning. I'm so glad you moved here. You're so good at distances. You're sure to win the cross-country run at the city invitational. You'll fly right past all those cocky runners who think they have no competition." Jillian leaned back and rested one arm up on the back of her chair.

Melinda raised her eyebrows and shook her head frantically, but Jillian kept talking about what a great runner Melinda was and how she's never seen anyone as good.

Melinda stood up. "We better get going. Glory is probably waiting for us."

As they walked past the other girls' table, the blond girl said, "Aren't you going to introduce us to your new friend, Jillian?"

"Sure, Ashleigh. This is Melinda." Jillian leaned forward, with her teeth together and an evil expression that surprised Melinda. Jillian's words cut through her slightly parted lips. "And she's going to kick your butt in November at the All City Invitational Meet."

Ashleigh cocked her head to one side. "Cute, Jillian. You almost look like you believe it. We'll see you there and see what happens, won't we?" Jillian waved bye to her dad.

Outside the restaurant, Melinda screamed, "What were you talking about?"

"She's a snob," Jillian said as they hurried to Glory's, "the leader of all snobs. She and her so-called friends have no right to think they are any better than anyone else. But they do. She always wins in cross-country. Her father was a great runner. Her older brothers always win. She really hasn't had any competition. She has to be beat."

"But, I'm not the one to do it. I've never raced anyone but my mom before, and that was just for fun. Sorry, Jill. I don't want to get in the middle of your little battle with what's-her-name."

"Her name's Ashleigh. Don't worry. You won't get in the middle. You'll just beat her and that will be that. End of story." The girls walked fast through the city streets.

The sun was low and their bodies cast long shadows in front of them.

"You seem to be forgetting one important fact. I probably won't beat her."

"Ha, you said 'probably'." Jillian stopped and faced Melinda, putting her hands on Melinda's shoulders. "You're good. I can tell already. You're a natural runner. My mom told me all about your mom, how she was the best runner in the city, but your grandmother would never let her be on the team, said it was not ladylike. Now, you can follow your mom's dream."

"What? How did you know my mom wanted to be on a cross-country team? She never told me that."

"She probably told you. I forget things my mom tells me all the time. You know parents start saying blah, blah, blah about their past, and we just want to shout 'Who cares if you had to walk a mile to school in a snowstorm along a railroad track and that you didn't even have computers.' The important thing is that you are going to beat Ashleigh. It's in your genes. You just may need a little practice."

"You're scaring me, Jill."

Glory opened the door as they approached the apartment. "Where have you two been? I told Charles we'd be there an hour ago."

"You are about to enter the world of snob kingdom. Beware," Jillian whispered to Melinda. "Now you should be scared."

Chapter 7

On the way to Charles' house, Melinda thought about Jillian and how she was glad to have made a friend so quickly. Maybe she would join the track team. She smiled thinking about how happy Jillian would be if she did beat Ashleigh. She'd probably do that funny dance again. Ashleigh might treat Jillian nicer too.

Glory drove Melinda past places that were already becoming familiar. She wondered if Mr. Jones was still working as they waited at the stoplight near Dairy Queen. As the car got further from Glory's, Melinda's heart beat fast and her stomach felt queasy. She was going to her new home to live with her Uncle Charles, who nobody seemed to like.

"I'm a little hungry. Do you think we could stop somewhere to eat?" Melinda said, hoping to delay the inevitable.

"Girl, you just ate enough spaghetti for three people. We're already late." Glory reached over and patted Melinda's leg. "It'll be all right."

They turned off the busy, crowded street onto a park-like boulevard with a grassy median blanketed in colorful tulips.

"This is Belle Meade," Glory said, "the neighborhood where your mother grew up and lived until she moved to Oregon."

Melinda stared out the window at the two and three story brick houses. They had large green front yards with tall, oak trees and perfectly groomed bushes. Flower-lined sidewalks led to stately double doors with brass-numbered plates and names such as Rockenfelder and Whitford. Each home had a three or four car garage, something Melinda had never seen in Shorewood.

"Wow. My mom grew up here?"

"Sure did."

"Only one family lives in each one?"

Glory nodded and stopped the car in front of one of the homes. "In some cases, just one person, like your uncle."

"My uncle lives here?" Melinda gaped at the building in front of her.

The huge house had green shutters on two stories of windows. Wide, rounded steps led to a front porch with white wicker furniture and a porch swing. A large weeping willow fanned most of the front yard. The sun had set, but the front porch light was not on yet.

"Your mama grew up here in this very house."

Melinda opened the car door and slowly walked toward the house. "Oh, my gosh. I had no idea. My mom came from a rich family."

Melinda suddenly felt sad again. These emotions seemed to spring on her and take over her entire body without warning or recourse. Her thoughts overflowed with questions. Why didn't she know more about her mom's past? Why hadn't they ever talked about it? Did she really even know her mother? She thought she did before she arrived in Chicago. Her mother never told her she used to drive or that she wanted to be on a cross-country team or that she grew up in a place like this.

Glory shut the trunk of the car. "Are you ready to go in?"

Melinda forced herself to move, to help Glory carry her bags up the steep steps, across the dark porch and toward the front door. Melinda's whole body trembled. She wrapped her blue sweater tightly around her.

Glory looked at her reassuringly and then rang the doorbell. Melinda heard heavy footsteps getting closer, the creaking of an old floor and a low, muffled voice. The door swung open and a man holding a telephone to his ear looked at them quickly and then turned and walked away.

"Yes, I'm still here," he said into the telephone. "I had to open the front door for someone. Now, go on. What happened with the Bartel's case? Hell, George. How in the world did that happen? I just don't understand the stupid-assed mistakes some people make. Where was Rebecca when this happened? That was her case. Now, they're probably going to sue the whole company."

His voice faded as he walked through a family room and a small door on the other side.

"Well, Mel, sweetie, that was your Uncle Charles, showing his true colors." Glory marched toward the retreating Charles. "Believe me, I'll have a word with him about this one." Melinda stood still, staring at where Charles vanished.

Abruptly, Glory turned back toward Melinda. "But, that can wait. Come on, honey, let me show you the rest of the house and your room. I know this place better than my own. You know, I added up how many years I've worked here, and couldn't believe it's been over 30 years. I've given this old house some of the best years of my life. Used to be fun when your mama was here. She was the cutest little thing. Those long blond curls and that sweet smile could charm a snake."

Melinda and Glory lugged the bags up a large, winding staircase, across a balcony to a room at the end of the hall all by itself. "You have a few rooms to choose from, but I thought you might like this one best of all." She stopped and pointed to the other end of the long hall. "The boys have rooms down there, but they're not here much since Charles and Renee got a divorce."

Melinda followed Glory into a room that was triple the size of her room in Oregon.

"This was your mama's room."

"My Mom's?"

Melinda paused just inside the doorway and scanned the entire room: white furniture with gold trim, a yellow canopy over a large poster bed, a desk with neatly stacked books, a pile of stuffed animals in one corner and an old record player in the other. Melinda slowly walked around the room, touching everything. She stopped in front of two doors which were side-by-side. She reached out and pulled back on the first curved metal handle. Inside, she found a yellow and white tiled bathroom with a separate tub and shower. Behind the second door, Melinda stepped into a large closet. Boxes were stacked on the floor, and girl's clothes still hung on one of two long rods.

"I cleared off the one side for your clothes," Glory said from behind Melinda.

Melinda caressed the sleeve of a blue sweater similar to the one she was wearing.

"Well, look at that. It looks almost just like yours."

Melinda held the sweater up to her face and cuddled it for several minutes. When she turned around to Glory, she had tears in her eyes. Glory hugged her tight. After a long silence, Glory said, "Maybe it will be too hard to stay in this room."

"No, I want to."

"Okay, kiddo, but if you change your mind, it's okay. Come on. Let's look around. It's getting late, and it's been a long day. I want to at least show you the kitchen. I'm in charge of stocking it. I hope I bought some things you like."

Glory showed Melinda the entire house. After seeing the four bedrooms upstairs, they descended the wide staircase and Glory pointed out Charles' room, the kitchen, dining room and a formal living room. All the floors were wood or tiled. They creaked as Melinda tiptoed past antique hutches brimming with delicate china and walls adorned with beautifully framed paintings.

"You don't have to be so careful," Glory said. "It's not a museum."

"It sure feels like it."

As they walked back toward the front of the house, Melinda heard Charles' voice getting louder. Glory knocked on a door to a room that looked like a cross between a library and an office.

"Charles," she yelled into the room. "You better get out here now." To Melinda, she said, "Sometimes I still have to treat him like a teenager."

As Melinda and Glory waited outside the arched doorway, Charles said, "Hold on a minute, George." Melinda watched him place the telephone on top of a large desk. He looked frustrated at Glory. "This is an important call, Glory. I have been gone for two weeks and the firm is in shambles. I need to. . ."

"Charles," Glory interrupted, first in a firm voice and then softer, she said. "Charles, I would like you to meet your niece Melinda."

Charles looked at Melinda, starting at her feet and going up until he finally looked at her face. Melinda felt self-conscious in her bell-bottom jeans with embroidered flowers she had designed herself, her purple tie-died shirt and ragged blue sweater. She slid the scarf off of her head before his gaze reached that high.

"Hello, Melinda." He cleared his throat. "Nice to meet you."

"Hi." Her voice sounded weak and squeaky. For a second, she thought about repeating the word in a louder, stronger tone, but she was afraid it would come out just the same, so she didn't say anything else, just looked at her holey tennis shoes.

Charles pulled his tan Dockers up, tucked his Izod shirt in and placed his hands in his pocket. He was a least a foot taller than Melinda. His hair was sandy blond like her mother's and his skin was tanned.

"I'd love to chat awhile, but I've been gone for a long time and I have some catching up to do at the office before I go back to work tomorrow. Do you mind? By the way, I'll probably be gone to work tomorrow before you wake up. I leave very early." He half smiled, first at Melinda and then at Glory. Melinda looked past him at the telephone still sitting in the same spot on the desk.

He did an about turn and strode across the room. Glory shut the door to the office and rolled her eyes at Melinda.

"It's a wonder I don't have more gray hairs," Glory said.

A few minutes later, Melinda was in her mother's old room alone. She listened to Charles moving around downstairs, creaking doors, sliding drawers, his footsteps getting nearer. The noise of the footsteps stopped at what Melinda imagined was the bottom of the staircase. Slowly, the sound of wood creaking got louder and Melinda knew Charles was getting closer to her room. She sat stiff on the side of the bed, not knowing what to do. While her heart pounded inside, she kept very still. His footsteps stopped right outside her door, but he didn't knock or say anything. The quietness of the large house vibrated in Melinda's ears.

She heard Charles clear his throat and then say, "Melinda?"

"Yes?" she managed to say.

"I'll be home late tomorrow night," he said through the door.

"Okay."

"Well. . . good night."

"Good night."

Finally, she heard the feet fade away and a door close beneath her room. She let out a big breath, and flopped back on the bed.

Chapter 8

When she awoke, it was light outside. She scrambled to her feet, glanced at the clock, dressed and made a dash for the front door. If she didn't hurry, she'd miss the bus and be late for her first day of school.

Melinda slammed the front door, jumped down the steps and ran the three blocks to the bus stop Glory had pointed out last night. She couldn't miss the bus. She had no other way to get to school. Being a new student was bad enough. Being a *late* new student would be worse.

She darted across the street, not hearing the car approaching behind her. The car honked and swerved, nearly hitting her. She stumbled, but regained her footing without falling down.

"Are you okay?" A woman in a black Mercedes peered through her car window. A teenage boy sat in the backseat looking out at Melinda. He had curly hair and piercing blue eyes. Melinda nearly fell over the sidewalk as she backed up.

"Yeah, I'm okay. I gotta hurry though. Sorry about that."

"You better be more careful from now on," the woman yelled as Melinda ran toward the bus stop, staying on the sidewalk this time.

When she rounded the last corner, she was relieved to see another girl waiting by the school bus sign. She came to an abrupt halt next to the girl, leaning over until she caught her breath.

"I thought I missed the bus," Melinda said.

The girl shook her head.

"Going to Roosevelt, right?"

The girl nodded.

"My name's Melinda. I'm new. Jillian, a new friend of mine, said I'd probably be the only one at this bus stop. Said all the kids in Belle Meade go to some private school. Do you know Jillian Jones? She just started eighth grade."

The girl shook her head again. Melinda was beginning to think she could not talk. Maybe she was deaf and dumb and was just reading her lips.

"How long have you been waiting? Are you sure you didn't miss the bus too?" Melinda looked right at the girl and spoke clear and slow.

The girl grinned and pointed to the big yellow bus approaching behind Melinda. After the bus screeched to a stop, Melinda jumped on, leaping over the middle step. She had never ridden a school bus or any kind of bus before. She scanned the rows of seats until she found an empty one and plopped down. The girl from the bus stop hesitantly sat beside her.

Melinda stared out the window at the passing houses. "They're mansions," she said softly. She was still amazed that her mother grew up here. Their house was about the size of one of these garages. They had no car, no manicured lawn, no VCR, no dishwasher or computer, not even a clothes washer or dryer. They carried their clothes in big duffle bags to the Laundromat six blocks away. They bought most of their clothes from the Salvation Army in Portland. Darcy would drive the one and a half hours two times a year, and the three of them would spend hours finding "treasures" buried in the racks and racks of used clothes.

Melinda watched the cars emerging from the big garages. Moms taking their children to the private school she guessed. Melinda counted two Jaguars, three Mercedes and one Lexus as the bus left the tree-lined neighborhood and entered the congested high-traffic street. She remembered all the afternoons she had spent with Darcy identifying expensive cars as they drove down Highway 101, strangers who visited Shorewood and then returned to their fancy houses somewhere. Although Darcy drove a beat-up Volkswagen Beatle, she knew all the expensive ones – makes, models and years. She could even talk about special features like turbo intercoolers and ABS braking systems.

"Well, that's really not that long of a ride, is it?" Melinda said to her seatmate as the school came into view.

"No," the girl said, surprising Melinda by speaking.

As they stepped down from the bus in front of the huge building, Melinda said, "Well, see you on the bus after school. I have to go find the office so I can check in, get my schedule, all that stuff new students have to do." She scanned the crowd of students all merging toward the front doors, trying to find Jillian.

"Can you point me in the direction of the office?" Melinda asked the girl, who hadn't left her side.

"I don't know. I'm new too."

Melinda noticed how the girl's lips quivered when she spoke, and how she fidgeted with her jacket buttons and looked nervously at the mob of students passing them.

"What's your name?"

"Emily. Emily Sanders."

"Well, come on Emily, we'll find the office together. Jillian said that this is a really cool school, and not to worry, but she's always saying that. Where'd you move from?"

"A small town in Tennessee."

"Oh, that explains your accent. I thought you sounded a little different. We're alike in a way. I moved from a small town too." Melinda looked at her new companion. They were also about the same height, but Emily was much wider. She swayed back and forth as she walked, and she touched her short black hair a lot.

Melinda noticed how the school building had several wings, and she figured the wings held all the classrooms and the office was likely in the middle since a principal would be better able to keep tabs on everything from the central location.

"This way," she said to Emily.

In the office, Emily shuffled her feet and twisted the front of her shirt into a big wrinkled mess. She reminded Melinda of a girl she knew back home. A lot of the kids made fun of her, but Melinda had gotten to know her and thought she was really nice, just not very confident. Melinda smiled at Emily as a secretary found their schedules, handed them a map and pointed them in the right direction.

As they walked through the now thinning crowd in the hall, they compared their classes and noted that they both had American Literature and then lunch together.

"I'll see you then," Melinda said as a bell rang and they parted. Emily looked as if she were about to cry.

"Don't worry," Melinda said. "Everything will be okay. See you in a couple hours." Saying 'don't worry' reminded her of Jillian again, and she searched the passing faces on her way to her first class. She glanced down to see what it was. Choir. How did she get in that class? She had always liked to sing in private, or in front of her mom and Darcy, but never in public. Fortunately, she didn't have to sing her first day.

After algebra, Melinda hurried to American Literature. She had thought about Emily the whole morning. As soon as Emily walked through the door, they waved to each other.

"Here, I saved you a seat," Melinda said.

In the lunch line, Melinda told Emily about her being in choir, of all things, and getting lost on the way to algebra. As they carried their trays to a table, Melinda heard someone yell her name.

"Jillian," Melinda said, "I've been looking for you all morning."

"I've been looking for you too. Here, sit with me. How's it going?"

Melinda introduced Emily and reported the details of her morning to Jillian and Emily. As she talked, she realized that she actually sounded like her old self again, and rattled on just like these were two friends from back home. After a good stretch of dominating the conversation, with Jillian periodically interrupting, Melinda concentrated on eating for a while.

"Melinda, you won't believe it," Jillian said. "I just sat by the cutest guy I've ever seen in my life. Look, look. There he goes. Isn't he a dream?"

After the boy passed, Jillian acted like she fainted and fell against Melinda. "His name is Justin. Justin and Jillian. Doesn't that sound like it goes together? Justin and Jillian. What do you think?" While her head was still resting on Melinda's shoulder, she looked up with her green puppy-dog eyes. She suddenly sat up and straightened her shirt. "Do I look okay? Did he even look this way? I didn't want to look and make it obvious or anything. Melinda, did you even notice? You were supposed to act like you were stretching or something, and look over your shoulder, like this."

Melinda said to Emily, "She's a little dramatic. You'll get used to it pretty fast."

"Hey, you got that from my dad."

While Melinda and Jillian talked, Emily seemed content just to listen and nod her head every once in a while.

Melinda told Jillian about how her uncle greeted her, his huge house, sleeping in her mother's room and almost getting run over by a car on the way to the bus. "Since you're obviously boy crazy, you'd appreciate this. There was this guy in the Mercedes that almost hit me who had the most beautiful blue eyes and curly black hair. I'll find out who he is and when you come to visit, I'll introduce you."

"No, thank you. I know exactly who you are talking about. Did his mom have black hair too, and a long skinny face?"

"Yes, how did you know?"

"Grams has worked there my whole life, remember? That's one of the reasons I know Ashleigh too. She lives in Belle Meade. Snobville. That guy is Bradley Rutherford. He lives right across the street from your uncle. I've heard Ashleigh has always had the hots for him. They'd be perfect for each other if you ask me, but for some reason, they've never gone together. Stay far away from all of them. They probably won't give you a second look anyway. They only hang with people like them, and you're not."

As the bell rang and they parted for classes, Jillian yelled, "See you in the locker room after school."

"What?" Melinda said.

"Cross country. Track practice. Hurdles. You're beating Ashleigh. Remember?"

"No, I forgot and I didn't bring anything."

"You're wearing your tennis shoes, and I knew you'd try to get out of it, so I brought you a t-shirt and a pair of shorts."

Melinda slapped one hand on her forehead. "Oh, brother," she said.

Jillian waved as she entered a classroom. Over her shoulder, she yelled, "You'll love it. Don't worry."

Chapter 9

Jillian was right. Cross-country practice was the highlight of Melinda's day. She ran the two-mile warm up with ease. Jillian kept trying to get her to run out in front, but Melinda wanted to run alongside her friend.

"Go on," Jillian kept saying. "I want Coach Robin to see how good you are. You're not even breathing hard. Go on." Jillian pushed her forward a couple of times, but then gave up after the first mile.

After the two-mile warm up, Coach Robin divided the team into their events. Jillian joined the hurdle group and Melinda the cross-country runners.

Some of the other cross-country runners groaned when the coach told them to run two more miles, but Melinda welcomed the opportunity.

"You can do it as easy as you want," Coach Robin told the moaners. "But you need to get the miles in."

The coach picked a thin, muscular girl with long legs to set the pace for the group. She told the girl to take the group through a trail at a nearby park and reminded everyone to watch for traffic crossing the streets. Melinda found a comfortable place toward the middle of the pack. About halfway through the park, Melinda looked up at the trees, not as tall as the ones back home, but still they reminded her all the times she'd looked up at trees while running over the years. She tilted her head back and breathed in the cool fall air, happy to let her body move in the familiar rhythm. She closed her eyes for a second just enjoying the moment, and suddenly felt a strong sense of her mother beside her. At first she was startled, but then a soft, warm feeling came over her and she ran with a new strength. She stretched out her stride, moved with more force and began to pass all the other girls, hardly noticing them. Once out of the park, she knew the way back to the school was a short straight shot and she pulled away from the lead runner.

Melinda ran onto the school track, not stopping until she came to the hurdles. Jillian was just finishing a series of hurdles. Melinda clapped and yelled, "Go get 'em, Jillian."

Jillian ran straight at Melinda and jumped up like she was mounting a horse. "I love hurdles. Mel, I owe it all to you." Melinda was caught off guard and they both went tumbling to the ground.

After laughing for a few minutes, Melinda said, "Please don't thank me anymore."

As the girls were leaving the locker room, Coach Robin patted Melinda on the back. "You don't know how excited we are to have you on our team. Jillian has told us all about you. She's right. Some of the best runners in the country have come out of Oregon. See you tomorrow, girls. Great to have you, Melinda."

On the walk to Glory's house, Melinda glared at Jillian. "What did you say to Coach Robin?"

Jillian grinned and started to run.

"I'm going to kill you." Melinda chased Jillian down the sidewalk. "What did you say?"

Jillian ran in between two buildings and disappeared near a community library. Melinda quietly peeked in between some bushes and then behind a large statue near the marble steps. A movement caught her eye. She tiptoed to the spot and then nearly fell over when she saw Jillian.

Jillian had somehow climbed into a large city trash container. Her legs were dangling out the front rectangular flap and her head and arms stuck out from the back flap. Her head looked like it was independent of her body, like it was resting on a ledge. She was making goofy faces, and Melinda fell against the wall laughing so hard she had to hold her side.

"You are the nuttiest person I've ever known," Melinda said. As she was talking, she realized Jillian was trying to get out. Jillian pushed up on the top of the trashcan with her arms, but couldn't budge her body.

"Hey, can you give me a hand?" Jillian said.

Melinda looked around. "I think I see that cute guy from school coming. What's his name? Oh, yeah. Justin. Justin and Jillian. Wait. He has a stack of books in his arms. He's coming right this way."

"Mel, get me out of here. NOW."

Melinda looked at Jillian. The trashcan said, "Thank you for depositing your waste here," in big red letters on the front below Jillian's feet that were now swinging up and down. Melinda began giggling again at the unusual site and had another uncontrollable laughing bout, until Jillian started rocking the trashcan back and forth.

"Stop. You could fall backwards. Okay. I'll help you."

Melinda slowly tilted the trash container forward until Jillian was able to work herself free.

"It's about time," Jillian said. "My butt was beginning to droop to the bottom."

Jillian brushed herself off and looked around. "You were lying about Justin. I should have known."

"I can't wait to tell Glory about this. If I only had a camera, that would have been perfect."

The two laughed and nudged each other playfully all the way to Glory's.

After a brief visit, Glory drove the girls home, dropping Jillian off first. As Melinda got out of the car, she asked, "Glory, did you pick my classes? The office said there was a form filled out."

"Yes, I did darling. Is everything okay?"

"Yes, everything's fine. I just wondered about choir."

"Do you like to sing?"

"Well, I do, but I've only done it around my mom and Darcy."

"Are you good at it?"

"Mom and Darcy always thought so, but. . ." Melinda stopped.

"What is it, dear?"

"Well, sometimes when I'd really get into singing a song, it made Mom get this weird far away look on her face. Actually, it happened quite a bit. It's another thing I wish I would have asked her about now."

"It might have just reminded her of something, or someone, she knew long ago. That's all. See you tomorrow, darling."

The house was quiet and Melinda was relieved when she found a note from Charles on the counter. He said he had a night meeting and wouldn't be home until late. She heated up a cheese pizza and took it up to her room to eat while she did her homework. She laid across the bed on her stomach reading from her American Literature book. She couldn't keep her eyes or her mind off of the closet in front of her. Finally, she closed the book and began to explore the contents of the closet.

She thumbed through a stack of worn record album covers. Elton John. Fleetwood Mac. Styx. Foreigner. Helen Reddy. The Carpenters. Bread. Some of the names were familiar because her mom had bought CDs of them. When she saw the pose of Carole King sitting in faded jeans, a wooly gray sweater and barefooted next to a window, she recognized The Tapestry album right away and a memory came flooding back to her.

A few years ago, her mother hadn't heard her come in the back door. The Tapestry album was blaring on the jam box. Melinda entered the kitchen area unnoticed and stood back and watched as her mother sang along. It was a catchy song about how she would always be around when she was needed, winter, spring, summer or fall. Her mother belted out the words with a wooden spoon as her microphone. She closed her eyes and wrapped her fingers tightly around the handle that was almost touching her lips.

Melinda loved seeing her mom lost in a song like this, but winced as her screeching words overpowered Carole King's beautiful smooth voice. Melinda began to mouth the words. "If the sky above you grows dark and full of clouds. . ." She could recite the words to the entire album in her sleep. She grabbed a spoon from the drawer and put her arm around her mother's shoulder. Her mother smiled, and they sang facing the back window that was dark now and showed a reflection of two female singers.

Melinda was so into her stage performance that she didn't notice that her mother had stopped singing. Melinda's body moved to the music. Her voice was in perfect harmony with the singer. When the song was over, Melinda threw her microphone over her shoulder and bowed a couple times. Then she noticed that far way look on her mother's face.

As she prepared for bed, she wondered who or what her mother was thinking about when Melinda sang. She decided to join Jillian in trying to find out as much as they could about her mother's past.

Chapter 10

Melinda fell into a routine of riding the bus to school with Emily, meeting Jillian and Emily for lunch, going to track practice after school, eating dinner alone and doing homework in her room in the evening. On the weekends, she hung out at Glory's apartment or Jillian's house.

One day Melinda helped Emily and her family landscape their yard. After watching Emily move big rocks around with her dad, Melinda came up with an idea. Within the week, she had talked Emily into joining the track team too and watched as the big, quiet girl held the heavy shot put on her shoulder, swung around and flung it several feet through the air. The entire team cheered while Emily shyly smiled and lowered her eyes.

With each cross-country meet, Melinda improved her three-mile time by a few seconds. During the last two meets, she splurged in the final seconds to cross the line first. Both times, she ended up on the ground afterwards when Jillian excitedly jumped on her. Emily was always there to lend a hand to help her up. Since track season was officially in the spring, all of Jillian and Emily's fall efforts were for the All City Invitational Meet, which would be held with several local schools in November.

While Melinda enjoyed being with her friends and Glory, she tried to stay away from home and her uncle as much as possible.

She and Charles communicated through notes they left for each on the kitchen counter. The first weekend, she found a note that said he was gone on a golfing trip and wouldn't be back until Sunday night. He left her "spending money," $20 tucked under the small piece of paper. The second weekend he left more "spending money" and said he was taking the twins to their "lake house" in Grand Beach, Michigan.

Twice, Melinda and Charles literally almost ran into each other in the kitchen. Once he was hurrying through to the garage as Melinda carried a bowl of hot oatmeal to the table for breakfast.

"Oh, hello," he said. "How are you?"

"Fine," Melinda said, standing next to the table holding onto the hot bowl until she hurried to put it down before it burned her fingers, almost dropping it.

Charles stared at her clothes a few minutes, and then said, "How's school?"

"Good." Melinda still stood next to her bowl, wondering why he didn't hurry out as usual.

He narrowed his eyebrows and pushed up on his glasses. "Why aren't you dressed for school? Aren't the

Rutherfords picking you up soon?" Charles pulled back his suit sleeve and looked at his watch.

Melinda's eyes roamed around the bright yellow kitchen while her mind tried to register the meaning of his questions. She had heard the name Rutherford recently, but couldn't think of where.

"What time do the Rutherfords pick you up for school?"

Rutherford. The boy with the blue eyes, in the car that almost hit her. Jillian had called him Brad Rutherford. He was her new neighbor who went to the private school. She glanced at Charles, who looked like he was about to lose his patience.

"Do you walk over to their house to catch a ride?"

"I catch the bus at the main entrance," Melinda said slowly.

Charles didn't say anything for what seemed like forever to Melinda.

"Oh. I see," Charles said as he brought his finger and thumb to his chin and looked up at the ceiling. "I understand now. I was in Australia. Glory didn't even ask about schools. She took it upon herself to sign you up for the public school. I just assumed you were going to Trinity. I assumed she worked it out with the Rutherford's to take you. A major error has occurred. Overstreets do not go to public schools, especially Roosevelt. I will tell Glory to draw up the papers for the transfer arrangements immediately."

Melinda sank down in the chair near her oatmeal. No. She wanted to yell at him. But she was afraid. She couldn't go to that private school, not after what Jillian said. Jillian and Emily would probably not even be friends with her anymore, and she would never join the cross-country team where Ashleigh went to school. They probably wouldn't even want her.

"I can't believe I've been so blind. The problem will be solved, no doubt."

"No," Melinda forced herself to say in a flat voice. "It's not a problem. I like Roosevelt. I like it very much. I have friends there. I'm on the cross-country team."

"No Overstreet has ever gone to a public school."

"I have. I am an Overstreet and I've always gone to a public school." Melinda's voice quivered, but she continued. "My school back home was a public school. Please, I do not want to go to a private school. I know I would hate it."

Charles took a deep breath and shook his head at Melinda.

"That's ridiculous. We'll continue this discussion more at a further date, but for now I have to make an 8 a.m. meeting." He turned and slammed the garage door behind him, leaving Melinda staring at her lumpy bowl of oatmeal.

She decided to pretend the conversation never happened. She didn't mention it to anyone, especially Jillian. She knew if she told Jillian, she would blow it all out of proportion and make Melinda worry about it even more. Maybe Charles would forget about it. Melinda took extra precautions to avoid Charles for the next couple of weeks. She was beginning to think he had forgotten it.

The second time she almost ran into him, she had been in the family room watching television and hadn't heard the garage door open. She usually heard it, and ran up to her room before he entered the house. This time, the first thing she heard was his keys being tossed on the counter. She jumped up, turned off the TV and almost knocked him over as he came through the doorway.

"Oh, excuse me," she said as she backed up to let him past. She swung her arms back and forth several times. "I just finished watching a show and was on my way up to do homework. Actually, I have my homework done." She worried that her mention of schoolwork would remind him of school. She quickly changed the subject. "I think I might go for a run, if that's okay?" She backed out of the room, and stood near the bottom of the stairs.

Charles just stared past her. "Sure," he finally said.

Melinda darted up the stairs, shut the door and leaned against it with her eyes closed. She stood there several minutes with her hands over her face. Then she changed clothes and slipped out the front door. When she was in the yard, she heard loud talking and the sound of a basketball bouncing across the street.

She thought about quickly retreating into the house before the group noticed her. She almost walked through the backyard, but changed her mind when she realized she would have to go through another neighbor's yard. She finally decided to quickly walk past the teenagers, and maybe they wouldn't say anything to her. She'd start running as soon as she was out of their sight. As she neared the Rutherford's house, everyone in the driveway grew quiet. The boy who was bouncing the basketball grabbed it and held it under one arm.

"Hey, Brad, why don't you introduce us to your new neighbor?" a boy said.

"She's kind of cute. You've been holding out on us Brad," another one said.

Just then, Melinda recognized the smooth, purring voice of Ashleigh. "Yes, Bradley, you haven't even mentioned her to me."

When she was next to the group, there was nothing she could do. She kept walking, but smiled slightly and said, "Hello."

Brad was closest to the road. He smiled back at her.

"We didn't actually meet that time my mom almost ran over you. I'm Brad Rutherford."

"Melinda Overstreet."

"These are my friends, Marcus, Daniel and Thomas. And this is Ashleigh Josten."

Melinda had no choice but to stop and acknowledge the crowd. Ashleigh had her hands on her hips and an obviously fake smile on her tan face.

"We've met," she purred. "I didn't realize she was your neighbor though. Bradley, this is the girl I told you about, the one Jillian Jones says is going to 'kick my butt' at the invitational. How odd that you are going running the night before the big meet. Our coach would never allow that, and I personally think it is a big mistake. But maybe you're desperate. Jillian does have quite the mouth, doesn't she?"

Melinda was speechless in front of Brad and his friends. She felt so alone and almost naked in her running t-shirt and shorts, standing at the end of the driveway looking at the group facing her, all huddled together, the boys wearing tan pants and collared shirts, and Ashleigh in a tight, knit sweater and stylish flared slacks.

"Oh, look at the time. Bradley, we better get going or we're going to miss the previews," Ashleigh said. She grabbed Brad's sleeve and pulled him back toward the house. He waved at Melinda before he turned around. "Have a good run," he yelled over his shoulder.

Melinda ran hard that night. She also ran longer than she intended. She got back long after the sun had set. As she approached the house, she saw the garage door open and Charles' little sports car back up and then whiz down the street, the red taillights getting smaller in the distance.

The next morning, she sat with Jillian on the bus to the All City Invitational Meet. Jillian bounced up and down on the seat. Emily twisted her shirt in the seat next to them.

"It'll be all right," Melinda reassured Emily. "You'll see." To Jillian, she said. "Will you sit still?"

"I can't. I have such a good feeling about this meet. I'm nervous, but I'm excited," Jillian said, twisting back and forth from her waist and then stretching from one side to the other. "I practiced hard all week, and knocked a couple seconds off my time. If I get the time I got Thursday, I could get at least second today. In an invitational meet! And my dad is coming. I want to win for him. Mel, do you think I have a chance of winning? Be honest."

"You just started this event a couple of months ago," Melinda said. "The real track season doesn't even start until spring. Think of this as practice for the real season."

"You don't think I have a chance of winning. Thanks a lot."

"I do. I do. I'm just saying if you don't win, you've still got the spring."

"Listen to you. You who just joined the team and are already getting first places."

"Jillian." Melinda shook her head. She didn't know what else to say to her friend. She was afraid Jillian would be heartbroken if she didn't place. She was afraid her friend would give up on hurdles before the real track season even started.

"Just don't be mad if you don't place. Winning takes lots of hard work and practice."

"Thanks for the vote of confidence. You're supposed to be telling me that I'm going to win, not preparing me to lose."

The bus pulled into a long, winding driveway. A beautifully carved sign announced their entrance to "Trinity – A school with a proud heritage." Flower-lined sidewalks connected old stately buildings that were surrounded by giant maple trees. Wooden benches and picnic tables made it look that they had entered a state park.

"This is a school?" Melinda said.

"Ridiculous, isn't it?" Jillian said. "Just be glad you are not going here. God, you would hate it, I'm sure. Everyone is so snoody. They're spoiled rotten. Wait until you see their track, and I heard the cross country trail is swept with a broom everyday."

The Roosevelt team exited the bus carrying their bags, walked beside a stone wall and under a high arched entrance into the stadium. Even though Roosevelt's team was larger, Trinity's side of the stands had more fans. Melinda's stomach suddenly began to feel queasy as she looked around. Trinity's blue and gold color-coordinated team stretched together in the middle of the field and the people in the stands sneered at Roosevelt's team as it made its way toward them. Several other teams were already warming up.

"See Ashleigh? She's front and center like always," Jillian said. "I can't wait for you to beat her. I'm going to be standing in front so I can see the look on her face as you break the line before her."

"Jillian, it might not happen today."

"Oh, yes it will. You can do it! You've been finishing each race faster. Coach says you are one of the best runners we've had in years.' Remember that your mom went here, and that being on a team was her dream. That will help you win. Don't worry."

The thought that her mother had gone to this school had been in the back of Melinda's mind, but Jillian's comment abruptly brought it to the front. Melinda suddenly felt funny inside. As her team walked past the Trinity fans, Melinda thought she heard her name. Then she knew she heard the name "Overstreet." She tried to keep walking, but the voices kept repeating her family's name, and she couldn't slowing down to listen.

"That's the Overstreet girl there," a man's low voice said.

"Her hair has that wild look like her mother's, just not as blond," a woman's voice said.

Melinda stopped, and pretended to tie her shoe.

"Shame she has to go to that school with all those kids. Look, she's one of the only white kids on the team," said a female voice.

"She's the spittin' image of her mother, isn't she?" said another female voice.

"I think she looks just like him."

"Oh, Claire, you don't even know who *him* is, and don't you pretend you do. No one ever knew for sure. That was part of the whole tragedy."

"I think he was that guy in the band."

Melinda gasped. Her eyes filled with tears. She stood up and started moving forward, and then turned around toward the exit sign, the bus and the way out. She bumped into the girl behind her. Jillian was talking, but Melinda wasn't listening, just watching her lips move. Other words kept screaming out at her. "Spittin' image of her mother. Looks like him. You don't even know who him is. Him. No one ever knew. Him. Part of whole tragedy. Him."

"Are you all right?" Jillian and Coach Robin were standing right in front of her.

"She looks like him. Part of the whole tragedy. Guy in the band." Melinda knew she had to have a father, but no one had ever acknowledged him, at least not to her. Did these strangers know her father?

Melinda shook her head.

"Where do you feel bad? Is it your head? Is it your stomach?" Brandy Lee was next to Jillian and Coach Robin.

Melinda nodded as she felt her world spin around. Voices kept getting louder then softer. People were walking, stretching, moving around her, but she was motionless, without feeling, just numb. Brandy Lee was taking her arm now, leading her to the car, helping her get in the car, driving her home, smiling uneasily at her, telling her she hoped she felt better soon, that she hoped her headache and stomachache went away soon, probably just the 24-hour bug.

"Hi, honey," Brandy Lee yelled across the parking lot as Jillian's dad stepped out of his car. "I'll be right back. Melinda's sick. Jill is so excited that her dad is coming to watch."

Her dad. The words echoed back to Melinda.

Inside her room, Melinda slammed the door behind her. The noise woke her from her trance. She looked around at her mother's belongings. "Why didn't you tell me more?" she screamed up at the ceiling. "Why? Why? Why don't I know anything?" She kicked a leg of the bed and threw a stuffed bear at the wall.

Suddenly, she heard a knock on the door.

"Melinda." It was Charles.

She wiped her eyes. "What?"

"I thought I heard someone yelling."

"No."

"Can you open the door?"

"No. I'm changing."

"Just wanted to let you know I've arranged for you to start at Trinity right after Christmas break. It's all settled."

Melinda swallowed hard and took a deep breath.

"Did you hear me?"

"Yes."

"Okay. Well, I'll be gone the rest of the day."

Melinda didn't answer and remained quiet until she heard the garage door shut and the hum of his car as it pulled away. Then she screamed again, louder this time. She banged on the bed until her fists hurt. She cried hard until she was all dried up, then she cried softly without tears. Finally, she laid her cheek down on the bed and whispered, "I just want to go home."

Chapter 11

The next day, puffy-eyed and drained, Melinda called Darcy.

"I have two questions for you. The first one is: Is there anyway I can come home?"

"I wish you could, honey. You know I do. What happened? Last time when we talked you were excited about running and your new friends and being in your mom's old house."

"A lot of things have happened. I hate it here now. I just want to go home."

"Did something happen at school? Did Charles do something? Did he leave you a nasty note?"

Melinda swallowed hard and couldn't tell Darcy about having to switch schools. She couldn't tell anyone. While she'd cried last night, she'd thought about her options. She could run away. But where would she go? If she went back home, they'd have to turn her in and she'd end up right back here. She didn't have enough money to go out on her own, and she'd heard about a girl back home that had terrible things happen to her when she'd run away to Portland. She'd love to move in with Glory, but she knew Charles would never allow an Overstreet to live in Glory's neighborhood.

Even though Jillian was right and she knew she'd hate going to a private school, Melinda realized she had no choice. She was under her uncle's care, no matter how much she didn't want to be. Jillian said everyone who went to Trinity was a spoiled rich kid. Melinda thought they'd probably make fun of her for not knowing her dad. They'd probably look at her like Charles did, like everything she said was stupid.

"I don't want to talk about anything here anymore," Melinda said. "How's work? How's Mr. Kolton? Seen Mack lately?"

"Funny, you should mention Ted."

"Who?"

"Mr. Kolton. Remember his first name is Ted."

"You call him Ted now? What's going on?"

Darcy giggled, and Melinda pulled the telephone back and made a face at the little receiver end.

"He's really a nice guy, Mel. He treats me special. We have fun together. I haven't dated anyone in a long time."

Melinda couldn't believe her ears. Darcy was dating Mr. Kolton, her own boss, her mom's old boss Melinda had known since she was a baby. He was fat and bald and boring.

"Isn't he a lot older than you?" Melinda said, trying not to sound angry and trying even harder to figure out why she was so angry. "What do you do together?"

"We go for walks on the beach. Rent movies. We've gone on two trips to Portland. He's my friend, Mel."

Melinda took a deep breath and bit her bottom lip.

"Mel, I'm sorry if this bothers you. It doesn't change how I feel for you, sweetie. I still love you very much and can't wait to see you again. Mel, what about you? Met any cute guys?"

Brad Rutherford's blue eyes immediately popped into Melinda's mind.

"No."

"Didn't you say you had two questions? What was your other question?"

"It doesn't matter anymore. It was a dumb question anyway."

"Come on, Mel. What is it?"

"Okay. Did my mom ever mention anything about you know who?"

"Who's you know who?"

"You know." Melinda was silent for a while. "Who my dad is?"

"Oh, Mel. I'm sorry you have to wonder about that in the middle of everything else you're going through."

"Well?"

"I'm sorry. I was nosy at first and asked her lots of questions, but she never answered me and it always bothered her so much when I asked, I quit asking years ago. I thought if she wanted to talk about it, she would.

But she never did. I've wondered ever since I met her. I wish I had an answer for you, but I don't."

Darcy talked about a diet program she was on and how she'd lost 10 pounds already. Before she hung up, she said, "Oh, Mel, this might not be anything, but your mom did mention someone she dated who was in a band. She said he had a beautiful voice."

• • •

Melinda thought about Darcy's last comment a lot and after a couple weeks, worked up her courage to talk to Jillian about it one day at lunch. Jillian was talking about the All City Invitational Meet again for the tenth time, saying how she could have won the hurdles event if she hadn't hit that last hurdle and how Melinda would have beat Ashleigh if she hadn't gotten sick. She said she thought Emily was changing since she won the shot put event, that all the attention was going to her head.

"Ashleigh strutted off the field after she won," Jillian said. "She has the tiniest little butt I've ever seen. She's a pole. Looks gross if you ask me. I bet she makes herself throw up just to be thin. I would bet anything. Girls like her always do. I bet half the girls at that school do. Can't you see them at lunch? Eating their salads with fat free dressing and then running to their sparkling clean bathrooms and. . ."

"Jillian, I'm trying to eat here," Melinda interrupted. "And I don't want to waste our lunch hour talking about what they do at that private school. Speaking of eating and Ashleigh though, remember our conversation at Dairy Queen that first time I met your dad?"

Jillian nodded. "What about it?"

"You said you'd ask your mom about, you know, if she knew anything."

"About what?"

"You forgot? Remember, it was something really important to me. We talked about it just after your DAD left the table."

Jillian slapped her palm on her forehead. "Mel, I'm sorry. I just got into this whole track thing and sort of forgot. I'll be spending a lot more time with my mom over Christmas break. I'll sneak it into the conversation. I promise. I'll let you know as soon as I find out anything."

After school, Melinda found a box with her name on it outside her room. She recognized the handwriting as she ripped the box open to see what Darcy had sent her. First, she read the scribbled note, "Hi, Mel. After our conversation a couple weeks ago, I went through your mother's things. I thought I'd remembered a box marked 'personal.' Thought you might find some clues to your 'big' question in here. Let me know if you find out anything. Love and miss you, Darcy."

Melinda lifted the smaller box out of the packing box and turned it around in her hands. It was no bigger than a shoebox, wooden with two hinges in the back and a piece of paper taped on top that said 'personal and sentimental.' Melinda had never seen the box before, but she did recognize her mother's handwriting. She slowly lifted the lid. The first thing she saw was a small stack of pictures. Melinda gently lifted the first picture and put it to her chest.

Melinda had been eight years old. Her mother was sewing at the table near her.

"Mom, when you get done, can I play beauty parlor and do your hair?" Melinda had said.

"Sure Mel, go ahead and get whatever you need to get ready. You can start on it while I'm sewing. I need to hem some pants, too, so I may be awhile."

Melinda reappeared from her room with handfuls of ribbons, bows, headbands and ponytail holders. She spread them out across the table next to her mom's sewing supplies.

"Do you want me to use a comb or a brush on your hair? Which do you like better?" Melinda had asked. "Act like you're really my patient, or whatever it's called."

Her mother smiled. "A brush, please, madam."

"How was your day?" Melinda asked professionally.

"Very fine, thank you. And yours?"

"Fine too. Thank you for asking." Melinda brushed her mother's hair and put it up in three ponytails, one straight out the back and one over each ear.

"Let me see, Madam," Melinda said as she walked around to the front of her mother. She cocked her head, put her hand to her chin and bit the side of her lip.

"How do I look?" her mother asked.

"I like this design on your hair. It makes you look younger. But, there's one stubborn piece. It's all right. Just relax," Melinda sprayed hair spray all over her mother's head, patting and spraying a clump of hair in the front several times. After her mother's hair was good and plastered, Melinda said, "Now, that's better. That stubborn piece is stuck with the rest of them now."

"How do I look now?"

Melinda stood only a foot in front of her mother looking intently into her face. "The style makes you look younger." Then she grabbed three lipstick tubes from her pile and held them in the palm of her hand. "Now, which color would you prefer, madam?"

Her mother looked at the orange, pink and red choices. "Well, I just don't know. Which color do you think would match my new hairdo the best?"

After a minute of looking back and forth between her mother's hair and her hand, Melinda picked out the red lipstick.

"Put your mouth like this," Melinda said. "Like you're saying yoooouu."

Melinda's face was only inches from her mother's now while she concentrated on putting the lipstick on. "This should look good on you. It's more of your lip color than the other two. Wait a minute. I smudged some." Melinda put her finger in her mouth to get it wet and then rubbed it around her mother's mouth that was now smeared with red lipstick.

Darcy had peeked her head in the door just as Melinda was finishing.

"Wow, don't you look lovely," Darcy said to Melinda's mother. "I think we should get a picture of this." Carole said no, but Melinda said it was a good idea.

Melinda now looked at the picture of her with her arms tightly around her mother's neck. Her mother's lips looked like red smudgy blobs and her hair stuck out like two stiff, straight branches, one over each ear. Their faces were cheek to cheek.

With a smile on her face, Melinda flipped through the rest of the pictures quickly recognizing days on the beach, parties at The Loft, her own kindergarten picture, her riding her bicycle and her blowing out candles on her 10th birthday. She placed each of the pictures around the mirror in her room, forcing them into the thin-rimmed crack so they would stay in place.

She was startled when the doorbell rang, but ran down to answer it, thinking it was probably Jillian or Emily.

When she opened the door, she was surprised to see two small boys who looked just alike running around a woman in a red dress.

"Hello, I'm Renee. Is Charles home?"

Melinda shook her head and the two boys ran past her into the house.

"You must be Melinda. I'm Charles ex-wife." The boys returned from behind Melinda.

"Mommy, can we meet our new cousin now?"

One of the boys looked up at Melinda, and pulled on her shirt. "Are you our new cousin?"

Renee pulled her keys out of her purse. "I'm sorry," she said. "I'm going to a Christmas party tonight and I need to go now. Charles was supposed to be here promptly at 5:30, but, of course, he isn't. Would you be a dear and watch the twins until he gets here?"

"There's daddy. There he is."

Charles's car turned into the driveway. He emerged from the low seat and strode across the lawn in his long gray wool coat.

"Got tied up at the office, but I'm only a few minutes late. Not bad."

Renee let out a loud huff and marched off to her car. "See you later, boys."

"Dad, can we meet our new cousin?"

"Yeah, Dad, can we? Mom said she lives here all by herself."

"Boys, she is not your new cousin. She is much older than you. And she does not live here all by herself."

"She doesn't?"

"No," Charles answered loudly. "I live here too."

"But, mom says you're never home."

"Well, I'm home now, aren't I?

Turning to Melinda, she said, "Melinda, these two boys are anxious to meet you."

Two pairs of wide eyes smiled up at her.

"Can you play with us, Linda?"

"Can I show you my remote control car? It's up in our room. Can we show you our room?"

One boy grabbed Melinda's right hand and the other her left. They started up the staircase pulling her as they went.

"What are your names, boys?" Melinda said at the top of the stairs.

"I'm Jake."

"I'm Sam."

The telephone rang and Melinda heard Charles answer it. A few seconds later, he yelled up the stairs, "Something has come up. I need to run back into the office. I'll leave some money on the table so you can order a pizza later."

"You get to be our babysitter," Sam said and jumped up and down and around in circles.

"We love babysitters," Jake said.

"Can we play horsy? Or cops and robbers?"

"I want to play war. I have guns and swords," Jake said.

"I want to play hide and seek," Sam said. He twirled his arms around like a helicopter.

Melinda started laughing. "Okay, we can play all those things I guess. First, you can show me your room."

Sam bumped into her as he ran past. "Last one in is a rotten egg."

"I won. I won. I won," Jake said.

"Linda's the rotten egg," they both yelled together. Inside their room, covered with airplane wallpaper and train sets and fire trucks, the boys picked up two big cars and made roaring sounds as they flew the cars around the room.

"Wow, you two can make a lot of noise." Melinda said. After a few minutes, they threw the cars on the floor.

"Now, let's go see your room." They both ran to the other end of the hall.

"How did you know where my room was?"

"It's the girl room."

Inside the room, the boys ran around picking up stuffed animals and photo albums and everything they could. They'd pick it up and then throw it over their shoulders. Melinda yelled, "Wait, don't pick that up. Hey, don't throw that, you might break it." Finally, she screamed, "Stop."

The boys got quiet and someone behind her clapped. Melinda turned around to see Jillian standing at the door.

"It was unlocked and no one answered the door bell, so I came in. Hi, Sam and Jake. Are you giving your cousin a hard time?" The boys ran up to Jillian and hugged her around the knees.

Melinda and Jillian played hide and seek, war and cops and robbers before the pizza arrived. Afterwards, they talked the boys into watching a Disney movie and then tucked them into bed. As Sam's eyes began to droop, he quietly said, "Linda, we forgot to show you the secret passageway in your closet."

Jillian and Melinda rolled their eyes at each other. "Another day, buddy," Melinda said, and he closed his eyes and fell asleep.

While Jillian put her coat on, Melinda said, "Don't forget to ask your mom to see if she knows anything."

"I won't."

Chapter 12

Melinda finished the fall semester at Roosevelt with mixed emotions. She felt good about her first cross-country season, her friendships with Jillian and Emily and the grades she'd gotten in her classes. Choir was her favorite subject and she continued to surprise her teacher and herself with her strong singing voice. The more she practiced, the better she could sing, reaching higher notes and holding them longer. During the Christmas concert, the teacher asked her to do a small solo part, and even though she was nervous, she sang loud and clear and received several compliments afterwards.

She was nervous and sad about changing schools. The thought bothered her so much she tried not to think about it most of the time. She continued to keep Trinity a secret, hoping to talk Charles out of his decision before the end of Christmas break.

The first Saturday during the holiday vacation, Melinda felt like running. She asked Jillian and Emily, but they said she ran too fast. She put on a pair of sweatpants, and doubled-up on top with short and long sleeved t-shirts. When she went out in the front yard to stretch, the wind wipped through her clothes and goose bumps spread all over her body. Her ears and nose immediately felt the winter chill. She stretched quickly, started with a warm-up walk and then jogged slowly down her street shaking her arms to the sides and twisting her neck to loosen up.

She jogged about two blocks and then picked up her pace. She heard footsteps fast approaching behind her, turned her head and glanced over her shoulder.

"Hi," Brad said, pacing himself beside her. "I saw you walk out with running clothes on, so I hurried and changed. Mind if I run with you?"

Melinda continued to run, but said nothing.

Brad said, "I like to run on Saturday and Sunday mornings, and it's nice to have someone to run with for a change. You have a pretty good pace for a . . ." He stopped.

"For a what?" Melinda said. "For a girl?" She looked sideways at Brad. He shrugged and grinned at her. He was slightly taller than Melinda and she noticed his black curls bouncing as he ran. He wore a sleek blue and gold running suit and matching sock cap, both had Trinity monogrammed on the front.

"You look cold," he said.

"I'm freezing. I'm running harder than normal to get rid of the goosebumps."

"Oh, good. I'm glad you're running harder than normal. I was getting worried I was losing speed or something. I usually don't have a problem keeping up."

"I heard you were a little conceited," Melinda said.

"What? Me? Who said that? I'm not bragging, I'm just saying you're a good runner and have a good pace."

"Now, I think you're a liar too. I've seen your times in the paper," Melinda said.

"Man, I'm striking out everywhere." Brad suddenly tripped forward and fell onto the grass next to the road. He caught himself with his hands and flipped around so he was sitting upright.

Melinda stopped. "Are you okay? Oh, my gosh."

Brad raised a hand and Melinda grabbed it and helped him up. He smiled and winked at her. She started running while he brushed off his sweatpants.

"I know you did that on purpose, but I can't figure out why," Melinda yelled as Brad ran to catch up to her.

"You said I was conceited. Would a conceited person fall on the ground while he was running, especially in front of someone he just met?"

Melinda just shook her head. "You're crazy," she said.

"Okay. I'll accept that description, for now at least. Turn on this street. I want to show you a path through a cool park," he said. "You'll get used to this weather. This is one of my favorite times of the year to run. You start out a little cold, but warm up fast."

They turned onto a street Melinda had never noticed. She saw the forest area a few blocks away. This was a great find. She preferred to run on trails instead on pavement.

"Why did you leave the invitational so fast? I wanted to see you beat Ashleigh."

"How did you know I left and how do you know I would have beat her? And, besides, I thought she was your girlfriend?"

"Your source of information is not very reliable, first the bad descriptions of me and now this. Ashleigh probably even tells people we are going together, but we're not. We do stuff together sometimes. Our parents really push it, but we're not girlfriend and boyfriend. Now, *she* is conceited," he said taking off his jacket and tying it around his waist while keeping pace. "I didn't know if you could beat her, but now that I've run with you, I think you could." They entered the park trail and Melinda's pace didn't slow down. Brad pretended to pant like a dog. "I usually have to slow down a little on the trails. Wait up."

She heard Brad slip coming up a hill. "I'm not falling for that one this time," she yelled back at him.

"I didn't fall. Just slid a little. Hey, you're good on these hills."

"Reminds me of home," Melinda said, beginning to get a little short of breath.

"I have heard that if you're half as good as your mom was, you could break school records," Brad said as he ran behind Melinda on the narrow trail. They weaved in and around trees and thick brush. "Follow this trail to the right and we'll end up where we started. I need to head back soon."

Melinda slipped the long-sleeved t-shirt over head and tied it around her waist, still running hard. "How do you know about my mom? Seems everyone here knows more about her than me."

"My dad told me. He was friends with Charles. He said your grandmother wouldn't let her be on a team, but in gym class, she smoked everyone, even most of the boys."

They came into the clearing breathing heavily. Their feet slapped the pavement in unison as they ran several blocks before turning onto their street. A woman Melinda recognized from the Mercedes incident stood with folded arms at the end of the Rutherford driveway. Melinda and Brad slowed and then stopped just in front of the house. They both took deep breaths. Melinda walked in long strides several paces and then turned back toward Brad. She twisted at the waist and then leaned from side to side. Brad cooled down by walking in a big circle in the middle of the deserted road.

"Heather, this is Melinda, Charles' niece from Oregon," Brad said as he let out another deep breath. "Mark was telling us all about her mom a couple nights ago."

Melinda furrowed her brow and wondered why Brad called his parents by their first names.

"Yes, Bradley, I remember quite well," Mrs. Rutherford said. "He seemed to be quite smitten with her. When we first dated he actually asked if I wanted to go see her star in a ballet. Can you imagine?" She turned and walked toward the house.

Brad looked at Melinda and rolled his eyes and made a face like he was talking like his mother, crunching up his nose and puckering his mouth. Melinda tried hard not to laugh by covering her mouth with her hand. Mrs. Rutherford snapped her head around and looked straight at Brad, who quickly changed his expression.

"Bradley, you need to get into the house and put some nice clothes on. We are leaving in a few minutes. I told you not to run today. I knew it would make us late, and it has. You'll have to take a shower and be in the car in 10 minutes or less." She flipped her long black hair around and marched in through the garage.

"What about tomorrow? Run again, same time?" He smiled, revealing perfectly straight white teeth. "You're good, but I know how you could be even better. I could guarantee you could beat Ashleigh in the spring invitational with just a few minor changes."

"Bradley James Rutherford," his mother yelled from somewhere inside the garage.

Melinda didn't answer Brad's question, but instead smiled and turned toward her house. When she opened the door, the telephone was ringing and before she could get to it, she heard the answering machine and then Jillian. "Melinda, I hope you are home because we are getting ready to pick you up for church choir practice. I also hope you remember that you promised Glory that you would be in the choir and sing at the Christmas program next week."

"Jill, I'm here," Melinda said picking up the telephone. "I'll be ready. I just went for a run. I'll take a quick shower and be ready when you get here."

"You forgot, didn't you?"

"No."

"Admit it."

"See you in a few minutes."

"Admit it."

"Bye, Jill."

On the way to choir practice, Jillian asked Melinda how far she ran.

"Just 30 minutes or so," Melinda said. "We ran through this cool park, Oak Lawn or something like that."

"Oak Dale," Jillian corrected. "Who's we?"

Melinda hesitated for a moment, and then said, "I didn't mean we. I meant I. Well, there was this dog that came out of nowhere and ran with me for a while. That's what I was thinking about I guess." She leaned over the back car seat and whispered, "Did you ask your mom yet?"

Jillian lowered her eyes, shook her head and said, "Sorry." She looked back up at Melinda. "I can right now."

"No." Melinda said softly. "I don't want to be here when you ask."

Since Glory had talked Melinda into being part of the Faith Baptist Church Choir, she always looked forward to the practices. She and Jillian were two of the youngest people in the twenty-member group. Melinda was also one of only four white people. Glory and her brother Leroy were two of the oldest members. They bickered back and forth and made everyone, including Melinda, laugh throughout the whole practice.

As the group was leaving, one of the members patted Glory on the back. "These girls are a good addition to our choir."

"They surely are," said another choir member. "Watch out, Aretha!"

"They're so good, I think they should have solos," Leroy said. The whole group was gathering around, nodding their heads and agreeing. Before the girls realized it, everyone had agreed that Melinda and Jillian would take turns singing the final song during the Christmas concert. While the lights were low and the congregation held candles, the girls would take turns singing "Silent Night."

Glory and Brandy Lee decided to celebrate the decision by taking the girls out for pizza. "It's about time you tried Chicago-style pizza," Glory said to Melinda. A crowd was gathered in the small waiting area of Uno Pizzeria.

"It's worth the wait," Brandy Lee said after they put their name in and then bunched into a far corner.

"I don't know if I'd say that," Jillian said as she looked at the group walking in the front door. Brad and Ashleigh's families approached the reception desk. After they gave their names, they turned around and saw Glory.

"Hello, Gloria. How are you?" said a man who looked like an older version of Brad. "It's always a pleasure to see you. How's Charles? Even though we live right across the street, I rarely see him."

"He's fine, Mr. Rutherford. Works most of the time. You remember Brandy Lee and Jillian."

Mr. Rutherford smiled and nodded.

"Have you met Carole's daughter, Melinda?" Glory said.

"No, but I've wanted to meet her," Mr. Rutherford said. "My, you look like your mother. It's a pleasure to meet you, Melinda. I really admired your mother."

Mrs. Rutherford stepped forward and wiggled her way into the small corner next to Mr. Rutherford and then said, "Bradley spent a lot of time with this young lady this morning going for a run through the park alone." She said the last words very loud, over the noise of the crowded waiting area, so that Ashleigh and Brad could hear behind her.

Melinda immediately glanced at Jillian who was staring at her with a hurt look. After a second, Jillian's expression changed to anger and then she turned her head.

The intercom announced that Glory's table was ready. Out of the corner of her eye, Melinda saw Ashleigh leaning in toward Brad, her mouth moving quick and furious.

Jillian barely looked at Melinda during the entire meal. All four of them were unusually quiet. "Guess we're all just beat from all this holiday hubbub," Brandy Lee said once, trying to justify the long, silent pauses in conversation.

Toward the end of the meal, Brandy Lee said she hoped Jillian's dad was home from work by the time they got home. Jillian looked at Melinda and Melinda suddenly knew what she was thinking. Melinda shook her head at Jillian, but it didn't do any good.

"Mom, speaking of Dad, Melinda has been wondering if you know who her dad is," Jillian said.

Melinda and Jillian stared at each other, and then Melinda lowered her eyes and dropped her fork on her plate. Everyone was quiet for several seconds.

"Melinda, I could tell you about the boys your mom liked when we were 13 and 14, but we grew apart the last two years she was here. I always regretted that. It was my fault. Kirk and I started dating, and I lost contact with my friends," Brandy Lee said. She let out a deep breath. "I'm sorry I'm not any help. I was just as shocked as everyone else. She was just gone one day. Next thing we knew, she was in Oregon and she had a baby." Brandy Lee looked at Glory who was nodding.

Glory stood up. "I'm tired and need to get to bed, beautiful ladies." As they walked out, Glory put her arm around Melinda, "Your mama was a beautiful lady, too, and don't you ever forget it." Glory lifted Melinda's chin with her finger. "Right?"

"I don't know, Glory. We were so happy, but now I'm so mad. Why didn't she tell me more? I thought we were close. Now, I feel like we were strangers. I don't know anything about her, or my dad."

Glory stopped and hugged Melinda tight, but the older woman's embrace didn't soften Melinda's feelings tonight. They stood in the crowded lobby again, but Melinda felt alone, her body stiff and her thoughts confused.

Chapter 13

The next morning, Melinda woke up early and decided to run before the scheduled time with Brad. It would cause less trouble if she ran by herself. After about two blocks, she was startled when he was suddenly beside her.

"Oh, didn't hear me coming this time, did you? I can be quiet when I want to. I thought we'd said 10 o'clock. I almost missed you. We usually spend the morning in church, but I told Heather I was sick."

Melinda glanced sideways at him and raised her eyebrows.

"Why do you call your parents by their first names?"

"I don't know. Always have. My older brothers do too. Most of the time I don't want people to know they're my parents. You know, like at the mall. You'll think this is funny. I was playing up the sick thing, coughing, lying in bed and speaking weakly. Heather said I probably caught something from you yesterday. She said 'Bradley James Riley, I knew that girl looked peaked last night.'" His voice was exaggerated and he had his nose turned up. When he finished, he laughed heartily.

Melinda couldn't help but laugh.

"Wow, I made you laugh." He ran and looked sideways at Melinda. "You have a big dimple in your right cheek and another one right in the middle of your chin." He put his finger in the middle of his chin, and Melinda automatically brought her finger up to her chin right in the middle of the crease.

"I like it. It's cute, kind of like John Travolta," Brad said. "That didn't come out right. I do not think John Travolta is cute. That was not what I was saying."

Melinda laughed.

Brad ran a step ahead of Melinda and then tripped forward.

"Oh," Melinda screamed.

Brad, who caught himself this time, turned around and smiled.

"Will you stop that?" Melinda said. "Why do you do that? You could really get hurt one of these times."

"Are you ready for a little running pointer, one that will make you so much better?"

"Will I be tripping when I run from now on?"

"Good one."

"Maybe I don't think I need any 'running pointer.'"

They followed the same roads they had taken the day before and entered the same trail. This time Brad went first on the narrow path. After a while, Melinda said,

"Not that I'm interested, but I bet you were going to tell me I swing my arms too much."

"No."

"That I need to keep my hips straighter."

"Nope."

Brad slipped up the hill again.

"That I don't slip up hills enough," Melinda said with a grin.

"Now, you are really funny."

They were both quiet through the rest of the trail. When they came back out to the road, they ran side by side again. "What I was going to say, not that you're interested, is that I think you would be even better if you straightened your back a little more, like this. It brings your shoulders back a little too. Try it." He reached over and touched Melinda in the small of her back as they ran. Melinda lifted and straightened.

"Can you tell a difference?" Brad said.

"I think I really can."

"Easier, uh?"

"Yeah, I think it is."

"Okay, now," Brad started.

"There's more?" Melinda said and raised her face to the sky.

"Just one other little thing. You have long legs. Your stride could be a little longer. Stretch out your stride. Try this far." They were both breathing heavy as they rounded the corner to their houses. He ran out in front. She tried to keep up and stretch out her stride. He quickly turned around and looked at her legs. "Swing your legs out way in front of you. Think of it as a big swing forward and then a swift kick back. There, you've got it. Wow. Look at you go."

Melinda ran faster and was exhausted by the time they reached their homes a few minutes later. It took awhile for them to catch their breaths. They both leaned forward with their hands on their knees.

"Great run," Brad said. He walked up into his yard and sat down to stretch out his legs. Melinda sat across from him and reached for her toes. When she looked up, he was smiling big right at her. She quickly lowered her eyes gripping the toes of her shoes.

"It's nice running with someone again," Melinda said. "Mom and I ran together all the time."

"Anytime you want, just let me know." Brad looked at his watch and walked toward the house. "I better get back in bed. Heather and Mark will be home soon. I'm about to make a quick recovery from this terrible illness that my evil new neighbor gave me."

Melinda crossed to her side of the street, and didn't notice Jillian and Emily standing in her front yard until she was a few feet away from them.

"Oh, hi," she said. "How long have you been here?"

"Long enough to see you with your new buddy," Jillian said. "And long enough to have a little chat with Charles who, by the way, mentioned that you will be going to Trinity next semester. When were you going to tell us?"

Melinda took a deep breath and looked down at her worn running shoes.

"First you lie to me. Said you ran by yourself yesterday. Oh, no it was with a dog, wasn't it? Well, in my book,

Brad is a scoundrel. But from the look on your face when you were with him, you don't agree. Now, you don't even tell me that you're going to Trinity. What's going on, Mel? Are we still friends, or what?"

Emily wrapped her coat tight and pulled down on her sock cap. She didn't look up at Melinda even once.

Melinda got ready to say "of course," but then remembered Jillian asking Brandy Lee about her dad when she knew Melinda didn't want her to ask while she was there.

Charles opened the door. "Melinda, you have a telephone call." He stayed in the entryway with the door ajar looking out at the three girls.

"Okay." Melinda shuffled her feet and swallowed hard. "Well, I guess I have to go."

"Yeah, right." Jillian said, and she and Emily walked out of the yard toward Emily's house.

When Melinda picked up the telephone, she was relieved to hear Glory's cheerful voice. She was calling to remind her of choir practice later this evening.

"Okay, I'll see you at six," Melinda said before she hung up the phone in the kitchen.

"I couldn't help but overhear," Charles said as he walked in from the living room. "I'm having a few friends over tonight for a catered dinner and I'd like you to be here. You can meet some of the students from Trinity. Brad Rutherford and his girlfriend and a couple other kids your age will be here."

"I really can't. I have church choir practice with Glory." Melinda couldn't imagine attending such an event. And, it would add more ammunition for Jillian.

"You go to Glory's church?"

"Yes."

Charles shook his head.

"I want you to be here tonight." He exited through the same door through which he'd magically appeared earlier. "And dress appropriately," he said from the other room.

Melinda phoned Glory to tell her the bad news. Glory said Melinda would be fine without practicing. Besides, they had two more practices before the concert. All Melinda could think about was Jillian's reaction. She could imagine the look on Jillian's face when Glory told her she wasn't coming, and was attending a party with Charles' friends. Jillian would probably say, "She's turning into one of them."

Upstairs, Melinda rummaged through her clothes trying to find something that was "appropriate." The problem was she didn't know what "appropriate" meant. She'd never been to a fancy catered party. She found two dresses that were still wadded up in a duffle bag. She thought about wearing one of them, but they were too summery. She kicked at the pile that she'd just dumped from the bag and discovered a wavy black skirt. She rooted around until she found a dark gray jean jacket. She put the pair on, and turned around in the mirror. Her belly showed, but only when she lifted up her arms. She only had running shoes or scuffed brown boots. She jammed her foot into the boots and to her reflection in the mirror, said, "It'll do."

The doorbell rang and she listened as Charles directed the caterers. She still had two hours until the guests arrived. She snuck downstairs to steal a Coke out of the refrigerator, but Charles saw her. He looked at her outfit from her boots to her belly that was showing now as she reached up to the top shelf. When he looked at her hair, she realized she hadn't brushed it all day, not that it looked much different afterwards anyway.

"I notice that you have changed clothes," he said. In the background, Melinda could hear the clanging of silverware and plates in the dining room. "I hope this is not what you expect to wear to the party."

"Excuse me, sir," said a woman in a fancy black dress with a white apron. "Did you want the green or red tablecloths? Also, we have another question in here with regard to the table arrangements."

Charles followed the woman out and Melinda hurried back upstairs. She shut the door behind her and locked it. As she walked past the mirror, she said, "Now, what am I going to do?" She tossed the pile of clothes on the floor around again, then went to the closet already knowing she didn't have anything resembling a dress in there. She pushed some of her clothes aside and noticed a big box that said "Sentimental Stuff" on it.

The small box of her mother's personal things Darcy had sent was mostly filled with pictures and ticket stubs from events since Melinda was born, but she knew this big box must surely contain more interesting things from her mother's earlier life.

The box was sealed with thick packing tape and Melinda had to find some scissors to open it. As she lifted the lid, her eyes opened wide. It was like finding a treasure box. She saw old report cards, pictures of her mother dancing, letters from an apparent pen pal from Italy, stories written for literature class and, most important, a diary.

Melinda delicately lifted the small gold book. It had a black nameplate that read "Five Year Diary." Above the nameplate in her mother's printing were the words "Carole Overstreet's." Below the metal plate, her mother had written "Private, Keep Out!" With colored pens, she had drawn and colored in a large flower with red petals that took up almost the entire front cover. She'd also drawn a small yellow sun in the top left corner. The seam was broken and two layers of thin cardboard peeked out.

Melinda slowly opened the fragile book. Her heart beat wildly at the thought of reading her mother's secrets from nearly 20 years ago. She might now be holding all the answers she'd been seeking. Melinda calculated that her mother's diary began about four years before Melinda was born. On the inside cover, her mother had written "Carole Overstreet, 13 years. 314 W. Belle Meade Blvd, 666-6887. Dorothy Overstreet, 49. Charles Overstreet, 50. Charles Overstreet Jr., 21."

As she flipped through the next pages, she skimmed the preprinted information about birthstones, holidays and horoscopes. Her mother had underlined her own birth month and sign: August and Leo. Melinda smiled at the thought of her young mother speculating about the supposed personality traits. "All are kind-hearted, generous, sympathetic, idealistic, executive and magnetic. Prone to anger and excess pride. Likes danger and adventure. In matters of state, bold and sagacious.

Happy in responsibility." Melinda nodded in agreement to most of the traits of her mother's star sign.

After gently turning more loose pages, Melinda finally came upon some of her mother's journal entries.

January 9 – Snowed! Got out of school two hours early. Great day!

January 20 – Stayed all night with Brandy Lee. Watched the Olympics. Did some prank phone calls on some cute boys we met in the mall. Hung up when they figured out who we were.

Melinda laughed out loud. She couldn't imagine her mother doing such a childish thing.

February – Had to miss a basketball game tonight. Bunch of girls from school were going. I had promised Mark Rutherford I'd watch him. But mom made me go to stupid ballet lessons. I hate dance. Why does she make me do it?

Brad's dad? Melinda thumbed through the box looking for a picture of a boy in a basketball uniform, but found none. She came across the dance picture again and studied her mother in the frilly pink ballet costume. Her hair was pinned in a bun on top of her head. Melinda had never seen it like that before. Her mother's long, skinny legs were crossed at the ankles and she was standing on the tips of her hard-toed shoes. She did not look happy. Her face was very serious.

Melinda jumped when she heard the doorbell ring. Her eyes darted across the room to the clock on the nightstand. It was time for the party.

"Melinda," Charles yelled up the stairs.

She threw the diary on the bed and ran over to the door. "Coming," she screamed through the crack. What was she going to wear? She looked down at her outfit. It wasn't so bad. Maybe she would wear it anyway. No, she wanted to stay on Charles' good side. She still needed to talk him out of sending her to Trinity, to show him that Roosevelt was a good school for her. She ran back to the closet and looked through her mother's old clothes. Near the back, she found several dresses, most looked outdated, but she let out a sigh of relief when she found a plain, straight black velvety dress with three-quarter length sleeves. She slipped it over her head and looked in the mirror. Her stomach felt queasy as she rubbed her hand down the side of the dress imagining her mother standing in front of the same mirror looking at herself in the same dress.

"Melinda, our guests are here," Charles yelled. Our guests? They weren't her guests. She looked down at her bare feet. She rummaged around in the closet for shoes, but only found a box of old leotards and tights. She quickly pulled on a pair of the black tights. Guests take off their shoes in fancy houses anyway. She reached for the door handle and then remembered her hair. Shuffling through some things in the top drawer of her mom's old desk, she found a black and gold hairclip and she pulled her hair back and put it up. Then she hurried down the stairs.

Several adults and teenagers were standing around talking in the living room and dining room. Melinda took a deep breath and entered the room. She couldn't wait for this night to be over. Several people stopped talking and looked at Melinda. She could feel her cheeks turning red and wished she could run back upstairs. Brad was the only person she could even imagine talking to and he hadn't noticed her yet. She spotted his curly hair with the group of teenagers in the far corner.

"Well, here we go with a few appetizers," Glory said bursting through the double doors from the kitchen into the now quiet room. Melinda was glad to see her, but looked curiously at her. Why wasn't she at choir practice? Glory winked as she carried the tray around the room. When she got close to Melinda, she said, "Thought you might need me more than the choir does."

"Thank you," Melinda whispered.

"You look beautiful, honey." Glory said, touching shoulders with Melinda and looking down at her dress.

"Thanks. It was in the closet upstairs. Must have been my mom's."

"By golly. You're right. I remember it. You know, it would be a good dress for the Christmas concert too."

"Except, I have no shoes."

Glory looked down. "Could be a problem. We'll see what we can do about that before the end of the week. Maybe you could wear some of Jill's."

"No. She's barely speaking to me anymore. Thinks I've turned into a snob."

Glory laughed. "Not possible. She'll come around."

Brad turned around and then left the group of teenagers in the corner to talk to Melinda.

"You look nice," he said.

"Thanks."

Ashleigh glided across the room and put her arm through Brad's. "Time to find a seat, Bradley." She pulled him away without even acknowledging Melinda. The teenagers all sat at the furthest table. Melinda wasn't sure where she should sit. She wanted to just grab a plate and take it back to her room. No one would notice anyway. She searched the crowd for Glory, but couldn't find her. She was probably helping prepare food in the kitchen.

"Oh, dear, Charles, you didn't tell me your niece was so cute," a woman in a low-cut, red dress had her arm around Charles as they approached Melinda.

"Melinda, this is Priscilla," Charles said.

"Oh, dear, it looks like the young people's table is full," said Priscilla. "You can join us, Melinda. We have a lot of catching up to do. I've been away on business for several months."

Throughout dinner, Melinda sat quietly. The four couples at her table talked about the economy, European travel and how busy the holiday season was for them. She could see into the kitchen from her seat and Glory smiled and winked at her several times. While dessert was being served, Priscilla directed her attention back to Melinda.

"Melinda, dear, I hear that you went to Roosevelt. What was it like going to such a dreary, dungeon-looking school?" Priscilla asked.

This was her chance to make the school sound better in front of Charles. "It's not a bad school at all. They do well on national exams," she said.

"That depends on if you call finally making it above the state standard 'doing well,'" a woman said and then laughed.

"If you liked Roosevelt, wait until you go to Trinity," another woman said.

"Charles," a man with a particularly low voice said, "hard to believe that a relative of yours, a descendent of the founding fathers of our school, would even consider going anywhere else."

"It was a mistake," Charles muttered.

"My hairdresser's daughter goes to Roosevelt," Priscilla said. "I am somewhat familiar with it. I hear it is dark and drafty, and there are lots of gang problems."

"I haven't noticed those things," Melinda said. "Roosevelt's football team has won state several times, and they have a great soccer team, and a great track team."

"That's all schools like that have to brag about," a woman said. "Sports, sports, sports. But what about academics or the arts?"

"Speaking of sports, Ashleigh tells me you are a runner, Melinda," said a man at the other end of the table. He and his wife leaned forward and Melinda got a good look at them for the first time. They were both tall and thin. The woman had short blond hair and a necklace with more diamonds than Melinda had ever seen. She knew at once that they were Ashleigh's parents. She wondered how much Ashleigh had told them. Had she told them what Jillian had said about "kicking her butt" at the invitational? Were the people in this room the ones who were talking about her at the invitational? She was surprised that the thought hadn't occurred to her before now. She suddenly felt embarrassed, and didn't want to talk at all anymore. She'd try to talk Charles out of switching schools another day. Everyone was still waiting for her answer about running.

"I'm just an average runner. I heard you are excellent and your sons are, too," she said to Mr. Jostens. Maybe that would take the attention off of her.

"And our daughter, don't forget," Mrs. Jostens began, glancing at the table in the corner where Ashleigh sat next to Brad. "We are known as the family of champion runners. It started when Russell was about Ashleigh's age. Right, darling?" Mr. Jostens took over the conversation and Melinda breathed easier. When no one was paying attention, she snuck into the kitchen and helped Glory and the caterers.

Melinda kept peeking out of the kitchen until the last guest was gone, then she said goodbye to Glory and started upstairs.

"Oh, there you are, Melinda," Priscilla said. Melinda hadn't heard or noticed them sitting in the living room, just off the foyer. "Come here a moment, dear. Charles, your niece is charming. She and I will definitely have to get to know each other better. Do you like to shop, Melinda?"

"I haven't done much shopping in my life," Melinda said, taking only one step into the room.

"Oh, dear, you poor thing. That will change from now on. Right, Charles?"

Charles made a grunting noise, then took another sip of his wine.

"We'll borrow his shiny gold VISA and fix you right up, Melinda. Have you ever been to the Fashion Mall?"

"No."

"Well, then, we're going." She leaned over and kissed Charles. "Lovely party, dear, but I'd better be getting my beauty sleep. Melinda, I'll give you a call soon."

Chapter 14

The next morning, Melinda woke up to Charles banging on her door. She rubbed her eyes and tried to focus on the clock. Did it really say 12:30 p.m?

"I'm leaving two packages outside your door. One was in the mail, the other just sitting on the porch. Glory said you were staying all night with her Christmas Eve. That's fine, but I want you to go somewhere with me on Christmas Day. I'll pick you up from Glory's. We'll be visiting your grandmother."

Melinda waited until she couldn't hear Charles' footsteps anymore, then she grabbed the packages and brought them in her room. One was from Darcy. The other Melinda couldn't tell. She opened Darcy's first. Inside, she found a large card with notes from several of her old friends and neighbors. Everyone wished her well and said Merry Christmas. She unfolded a piece of lined paper with Darcy's handwriting.

Hi Mel,

I'm glad you sounded better on the phone last week and that you liked the box of personal items I sent. Well, you won't believe this. Sit down now (if you're not already). Ted proposed to me on a starry night on the beach. We're getting married in Reno on New Year's Day. Corny I know. Mel, he makes me so happy. He said I didn't have to waitress anymore. I'm going to take accounting classes in Astoria so I can help with payroll and bookkeeping. And, he is flying me to see you for your birthday in May. Won't you be graduating from 8th grade then too? Maybe, I can make it for that too. Hard to believe you'll be in high school soon. I can't wait to see you. I'm proud of how good you're doing there. Your mom would be too. Think we can ride in a taxi in downtown Chicago? I love and miss you,

Darcy

Melinda folded the letter back up and held it in her hand for a long time. Darcy sounded different. She didn't say she was sorry all the time. She didn't say bad things about herself. She didn't ask Melinda's opinion about anything anymore. She'd lost weight. Melinda didn't even know if she'd recognize her when she came to visit. She knew Darcy sounded happy, but she didn't want Darcy to change.

Slowly, she opened the two presents. The first was a light blue sweatshirt that said "Shorewood Beach, Oregon" and showed seagulls flying over the waves and Sally's Rock. Melinda missed that beach, the sound of waves, the smell of salt in the air, and the sand beneath her feet. The second was a framed picture of the three of them on the beach just a few weeks before her mother died. Tears fell down Melinda's cheek and she wiped them away with her sleeve.

She picked up the other package. A card on the top had a cartoon Santa in a jogging suit. Inside, it was signed, "Merry Christmas. My dad runs a wholesale shoe business. Thought you might enjoy some new running shoes. Saw your size when we were stretching. Brad."

Melinda heard the door open downstairs and then Jake and Sam's voices. They ran upstairs and burst into her room.

"Hey, guys."

"Why are you still in your pajamas?"

"Will you play with us?"

"Boys," Charles yelled from downstairs.

"Let me change and then I'll play."

Melinda spent the day with the boys. Charles surfaced from the office every couple of hours to get another cup of coffee. When the twins left that evening, Melinda searched her room for her mother's gold diary. The room was messy. Clothes, some clean, some dirty, were strewn all over the floor. The comforter was falling off the bed. Old plates and glasses were on the nightstand and the desk. The room was in disorder before the twins arrived, but after they paraded through it several times, it looked even worse. She couldn't find the diary anywhere. She picked up the black dress and hung it back in the closet. Then, she spent the entire evening cleaning up her room. But she never found the diary.

The next morning, she looked all over the boys' room, and then went from room to room, lifting up pillows and looking under beds and chairs. Glory picked her up in the afternoon, and they went to choir practice together. Jillian was civil, but treated her like someone she hardly knew. Just before they sang "Silent Night," Jillian mumbled, "New tennis shoes."

Melinda spent the evening helping Glory wrap presents, bake cookies and cook for her Christmas Eve dinner the next day.

On the morning of the 24th, they practiced their Christmas program for the last time. As Melinda and Jillian finished "Silent Night," the choir gave them a standing ovation and said it was the most beautiful version they'd ever heard.

Melinda spent Christmas Eve with Glory and her family. At midnight, Glory, Leroy, Jillian, Melinda and the other 16 members of the Faith Baptist Church filled the small, modest church with music. Melinda stood on the stage in her mother's black dress and a new pair of shoes from Glory. She sang like she'd done for her mother and Darcy so many times, but now to a much larger audience. To her it didn't matter if it was two people or two hundred, singing had always made her feel good. She forgot everything else and concentrated on the words and her changing pitch. The congregation applauded loudly after each song. Several choir members had solo parts and Melinda marveled at the range in their voices.

Just before "Silent Night," the preacher gave a short sermon while parishioners passed out candles to each person. After a prayer, the lights were turned off, and

Melinda felt mesmerized by the sea of shimmering lights and the closeness of the congregation before her and of the choir members beside her. As the piano signaled the start of "Silent Night," she closed her eyes and her voice flowed from her body, ringing out the words to the familiar song with a new energy and confidence that came from somewhere deep and warm within her. Jillian sang her solo part and then the two finished the song together in perfect harmony. Their eyes locked for a moment and they smiled.

When everyone walked out of the church, the ground was blanketed with snow. The sky was a changing curtain of falling white powder. "This is amazing," Melinda said to Glory. She held out her tongue to catch a snowflake. "My mom told me about nights like this. Look at the street lights, how the snow looks around the light. Wow."

Chapter 15

On Christmas Day, right in the middle of a huge Christmas feast at Glory's, Charles pulled up outside the apartment and honked several times. Glory looked disgusted. Melinda reluctantly put her coat and hat on and said goodbye.

She climbed into Charles' black BMW. He was on his cell phone. "Yes, Priscilla, I'll meet you at 7:30 at Basil's. Yes, I remembered the bottle of wine. Yes, I just picked up Melinda. No, I'm not angry at you. I just hate going to see my mother. It's depressing. Bye, dear."

Charles glanced toward Melinda who had his briefcase on her lap. "Oh, you can put that in the back. Glory's was fine, I presume. Carole always spent a lot of time there, much to Mother's dismay."

Melinda imagined her mother sitting in Glory's kitchen helping peel potatoes. That was one piece of history about her mother that didn't surprise her.

"Know anything about Alzheimer's?"

"A little," Melinda said. "Old people get it. They start forgetting things, simple things like where their bedroom is in the house. They can't even remember their own families sometimes."

"Sounds like you know a lot about it."

"I did a paper on it for school last year."

"Well, okay then. You'll understand even more when you meet your Grandmother Overstreet in a few minutes."

Melinda smiled to herself. She had met her grandmother before, years ago, just before she became ill. It took Melinda awhile to get used to her brash ways, but once she got to know her, Melinda enjoyed her company and found her grandmother to be a funny, entertaining woman.

Charles turned on the radio, but after two Christmas songs, he turned it off. He thumped his fingers on the stick shift, then rummaged through the console, found a jazz CD and slid it in the player. Melinda looked out her window. Christmas lights were everywhere. They drove into a residential neighborhood and stopped in front of a big white house. A wooden white sign in the middle of the yard said "The Bartley House." White lights lined the long front porch and Charles walked through the double doors without ringing the doorbell.

"Come in," he urged to Melinda, who had stopped just inside the door.

They entered into a large, open room. They were the only ones there, and it looked like an expensive, old house, not a place for sick people. The tan room with white trim smelled like lemon cleaner. An instrumental version of "Away in a Manger" played in the distance.

Charles walked to a chair in the corner and sat down, motioning for Melinda to sit across from him.

"Living so far away and under the circumstances, you didn't know Mother," Charles said fidgeting in his seat. He always presumed things, Melinda thought, never asked questions. "You'll see her in a minute, but it's not really her. Not like she was. She can't remember if I came to see her yesterday or a year ago." Charles talked in short, fast bursts. "When we get into her room, don't say anything. Let me do all the talking. I just wanted you to know, or at least see, who your grandmother was. She's deteriorating rapidly."

He wiped his palms on the wood-grained arm of the chair, looked at the dark streaks, and then rubbed his hands on his black slacks. He stood up, took his jacket off, draped it over his arm and loosened his tie. He paced back and forth. "This place is always so hot. Where's Mrs. Shelly, anyway? She usually comes as soon as she hears the door." He leaned toward the hallway and yelled, "Mrs. Shelly!"

A smiling black woman in a Christmas sweater and matching green slacks appeared. Charles quickly introduced Melinda and said they were ready for Mother. Beads of sweat formed on Charles's forehead. He wiped them with his fingers and slung his hand toward the floor. Melinda studied his behavior curiously.

In a moment, two women approached the room. Mrs. Shelly was talking to a tall, thin silver-haired woman in a silky green dress. "I know we need to fix that, Mrs. Overstreet. We are working on it, I promise you."

"At this rate, I'll be back home before it's fixed. You know I'm going home soon. I was just looking for a cab service in the telephone book." Mrs. Overstreet stopped talking. "Where is everybody? This place is too quiet."

"Remember, Mrs. Overstreet. A lot of people went home for the holidays . . ."

"Oh, yes, I remember, of course. That's what I intend to do today, too."

Mrs. Shelly cleared her throat. "Look, your son has come to see you, Mrs. Overstreet."

"Charles. Good. You know I was just going to call a cab. I am ready to go home, Charles. I do not want to stay here another day." Without looking up, she turned and marched back down the hall toward her room. "Come, Charles. Help me pack." Charles caught up to his mother and walked closely behind her. Melinda cautiously followed, looking in all directions at the unusual facility. As she passed the rows of doors, she glanced inside one that was open. An old man appeared to be dozing in a rocking chair next to the window. He rocked back and forth with his head turned toward the paneled glass. Melinda wondered if he could see outside or just the reflection of his room like she did.

"Mother. Mother. Slow down, Mother. It's Christmas Day. No one can check out now."

"Why not?" Mrs. Overstreet yelled from inside the room as Charles entered.

Melinda stopped at the doorway to the small, apartment-like space. She stood there looking at the twin-sized bed, nightstand, side chairs, dresser and entertainment center. The television was on, but the volume was turned down low. *Redbook* and *Ladies' Home Journal* were fanned across the end table. The room smelled like evergreen air freshener.

Mrs. Overstreet pulled clothes out of the dresser and neatly stacked them in piles on the bed. Charles bent down and kissed her on the cheek. "Merry Christmas, Mother. Don't worry about this now. We'll discuss it next time. It's not possible to leave today. The doctor told me you may be ready to go home in a few weeks. I brought you something. A Christmas gift, Mother. " Charles picked up a stack of nylons and placed them back in a drawer.

"No doctor knows what's best for me." She folded a nightgown on top of a housecoat, took a step backward and with her right hand, guided herself into the nearest chair. Melinda watched from the door, afraid to make any noise. Her grandmother looked frail and bony. Her breathing was slow and heavy and she stared at a spot on the carpet for a long time before she looked up at Charles now sitting in the chair near her. He reached into his shirt pocked and handed his mother a small wrapped gift.

"I hate those dizzy spells. Charles, dear, have you gained weight?" Her head bobbed like it was too heavy to keep up. "Lost some more hair? Something is different. Your face is red. Have you been drinking again? You know how I hate that stuff. Look at that poor excuse for a Christmas tree." She pointed with a long, skinny finger to a silver tree atop a draped table in the corner. "Puny thing, isn't it? Hardly an ornament on it. You know I'm probably paying this place a lot of money for that. It's pathetic. I'm paying for the foul-smelling air freshener they use in here too. I've always hated air fresheners. Give me a headache." She lowered her head and took a couple of deep breaths.

"Here, Charles. Now let me see what you brought me. I hope it's not another fruitcake. The staff here has given me two already. Do I look like I like fruitcake? Or chocolate covered cherries? That's another favorite people like to give old folks. I'm going to place all their fruitcakes and chocolate covered cherries on the top of my trashcan so they get the message. Charles, why haven't you been to see me in so long?"

Melinda smiled. Some parts of her grandmother had not changed.

"Mother, it's not a fruitcake or cherries, and I was just here, a few days ago." He pushed the box toward her on the small table between them. Melinda leaned against the doorframe. Charles seemed to have forgotten she was there.

"Charles, I'm not the fool you think I am. I know I can't remember everything, but I'm still here, Charles. I need a blanket over my legs. There's a draft in this room. Did you leave the door open?" Charles and Mrs. Overstreet both looked toward the door and at Melinda.

"Oh, dear, Charles. Did you bring someone with you and didn't tell me?"

Charles nodded. "Yes, Mother. I did."

Mrs. Overstreet smoothed her hair back and straightened out her dress. With some effort, she rose and made her way across the room to Melinda. Her gray eyes watered over and her lips began to quiver. She brought her bony fingers over her o-shaped mouth.

"Oh my, Charles. You brought my girl, Charles. You brought my baby." Tears slid from her eyes and rolled over her wrinkled cheekbones. "Come here and give your mother a hug."

Charles shook his head and looked up at the ceiling.

Melinda did as she was told and hugged her grandmother's frail body. She felt the woman's thin arms wrap around her waist.

"Carole, have you been on a diet again? You're not eating enough, I can tell. I told you being a vegetarian was not good for you." She stepped back from Melinda and studied her. "Doesn't she look thin, Charles? Tell your sister she needs more protein. Take that ponytail out of your hair." Before Melinda could move, Mrs. Overstreet reached up and pulled the band from Melinda's hair. "Your hair's lighter and straighter, too. Still stringy though. Put that back in, Carole, dear."

"I am not. . ." Melinda began. Charles waved his arms high in the air behind his mother's back. Wide-eyed, he shook his head in tiny jerks.

"Mother, will you please come open your present? I can't stay long. Mother, please. Look here." He tried to turn her away from Melinda, then he motioned for Melinda to leave the room.

"Where are you going?" Mrs. Overstreet said to Melinda. "You just got here. Have you seen the keys to my Cadillac? I've been looking for them all day."

Melinda looked back and forth between her uncle and her grandmother. "Grandmother, I'm Melinda. Remember me? Remember when you came to see me and mom two years ago? You were there for my 12th birthday. Remember our house near the beach, our long walks on the sand?" Melinda stopped for a second, smiling at a memory forming in her mind. Mrs. Overstreet tilted her head and gazed at the corner of the room. Melinda laughed. "Remember how I taught you to fly a trick kite and you almost killed that guy lying on the beach. Hit him right on the middle of the back with the point. Mom and I couldn't stop laughing. You laughed, too, after we found out the guy was okay."

Mrs. Overstreet's eyes began to focus on a watercolor painting above her bed. She smiled but was silent for several minutes. Melinda didn't know what to say. Charles stood up and marched toward Melinda. He leaned over and whispered in her ear. "I don't know why you're making up this story. Carole left Mother and Father when she was very young. It hurt them very much. They never visited her. The only time Carole came home was when Father died. This is not good for her. Go wait in the lobby."

"Hush, Charles," Mrs. Overstreet snapped. She turned around and looked right at him. "You think I can't hear you? You think I'm already gone. Well, I'm not. Why don't you go wait in the lobby? Come over here and sit by me, child." She looked clearly at Melinda for the first time. Their eyes locked, one pair worn and weathered in sunken, wrinkled sockets, the other brighter, energetic and eager.

Mrs. Overstreet smiled and talked slow. "I do remember now. I did go, Charles. I don't tell you everything. Never did." Mrs. Overstreet turned toward Charles. "I knew I was getting sick and you were talking to doctors about what to do with me. Some days, I was aware of everything. I talked to the doctor, too. He said I had time, a little at least, to tie up some loose ends." She swallowed hard and licked her cracked lips. Her head fell down and then she lifted it toward Melinda. "I went to Carole to say I was sorry, sorry for being a bad mother. I realized I tried to make her into something she wasn't. I told her I was sorry for running her off when she needed me most. Sorry for saying she'd been reckless." She reached up and touched Melinda's cheek, and then cupped her granddaughter's chin in the palm of her hand. "I did a terrible thing. I accused her of being a drunk driver. Said her own stupidity had killed those people. I did a terrible thing." She looked down then, shaking her head. Melinda's eyes widened. What in the world was she talking about?

"It was just an accident," Mrs. Overstreet continued. "I pushed my baby away when she was just a girl. She was pregnant, too, and I didn't even know it."

Mrs. Overstreet's shoulders drooped low and she began to cry. Charles handed her a handkerchief from his pocket. She wiped her eyes and then smiled at Melinda.

The old woman reached for Melinda's hand and brought it to her lap, then sandwiched it between her own leathery fingers. Her smile grew wider. "I remember my glorious visit. I remember your cottage by the ocean, your birthday and my horrendous kite lesson. That young fellow, lying peacefully on his stomach, arched his back as the kite jabbed him right on the spine." A laugh escaped just before she covered her mouth with her hand. "I was afraid I'd really injured him. He was so noble about the whole thing. Oh, how we laughed. That was one of the best weeks of my life." With a tilt and slight toss of her head, she motioned toward the other side of the room. "You know I've kept every letter you and Carole sent me since that visit. They're all over there." She pointed to a ceramic box on the nightstand. "Where is my Carole?"

She suddenly stood up, made her way to the door and opened it. She looked down the long hallway. "Okay, Carole, you can come in now." She smiled back at Melinda.

"My mother's not here," Melinda said. Charles cleared his voice. His jaw was tight and he shook his head in long, slow motions from side to side. *She doesn't even know,* Melinda thought.

"Where is she, dear?"

Charles stood, crossed the room and started to close the door. "She's back in Oregon. She wasn't able to come," he began. "We really need to go now."

Melinda lowered her head and sank deeper into the chair.

Mrs. Overstreet stood frozen near the door. "Where is she, dear?" She looked from Melinda to Charles and then back at Melinda. "You can tell me."

Slowly and softly, Melinda answered. "My mother died in August, in an accident on her bicycle."

Her grandmother began to sway. Her head fell back. She caught herself against the wall. Melinda and Charles rushed to help her cross the room and lie down on the bed. Before her head reached the pillow, she grabbed Melinda and held her tight. They embraced and sobbed in the small room. Charles stood next to them with a stiff arm braced against the wall, staring out the dark window, his reflection taking up most of the glass.

Mrs. Overstreet finally pulled her head back from Melinda, but still clung to the girl's body. Her moist gray eyes were glazed again and she stared past Melinda, over her shoulder at a spot on the wall. In the hall, sounds of Mrs. Shelly helping another patient return to her room echoed and seeped through Mrs. Overstreet's crowded space.

Melinda kept thinking back to something her grandmother had said. "Grandmother, what did you mean by saying you were sorry for saying my mom was a drunk driver? And what about killing people and it being an accident? My mom never killed anyone. She would have told me that."

Without looking at Melinda, Charles answered in a dull, flat voice. "Mother is out of it again. I can tell by the look in her eyes. The people who died were friends of your mother. Some people blamed her, but it was an accident. Carole wasn't drunk. It was just a really bad accident. She went 2,000 miles away to escape the tragedy."

Mrs. Overstreet rubbed Melinda's arm and wept, "Carole, my beautiful Carole. It was my fault you ran away. I know I don't deserve it, but will you ever forgive me? Will you, dear?"

The room began to spin around Melinda. She felt lightheaded as memories of her mother rushed past. Things made sense now – her mother not driving, not drinking and not keeping in touch with her family. She'd found pieces to a puzzle she didn't even know were missing, until now.

Suddenly, Melinda had to sit down. Her grandmother was still hanging onto her, and the weight became unbearable. She carefully removed herself from the tight grip, and the elderly woman's head rested on the pillow. After sliding a stack of clothes over on the bed, Melinda sat next to her grandmother whose eyes were now shut.

Charles looked at his watch, took a deep breath and then grabbed the present on the table. "Mother, we need to leave in a minute. Visiting hours are almost over. Do you want to open your Christmas present while I'm here?"

Mrs. Overstreet didn't move for a long time. Charles looked up at the ceiling again and shook his head. He muttered to himself, "God, I hate this place. I've got to get out of here. Hope you like the necklace." He started for the door.

Mrs. Overstreet half opened one eye. "Charles, dear. I can't find my keys. Do you mind driving?" Charles groaned and ran his fingers through his thinning hair. Someone knocked on the door and Mrs. Shelly announced, "Visiting hours are over."

Charles flung the door open. "Mrs. Shelly, could you please help Mother put her things away and get ready for bed?" He walked to his mother's side, kissed her on the cheek and said, "Good night, Mother. You're getting tired and I need to get home. I'll visit again soon. Merry Christmas."

With a jerk of his head, he motioned for Melinda to follow him to the door. She took two tiny steps toward Charles, but then turned and ran back to her grandmother. She sat on the bed, pulled the limp body close and held her.

"Good night, Grandmother," she whispered. "Mom forgave you long ago."

Chapter 16

For the next three days, Melinda could think of nothing but what her grandmother and Charles had said about her mother. She kept replaying the conversation like a recording in her mind: when she'd get to the end, she'd hit rewind and play it again. Her mother was driving, got in an accident and some friends of hers were killed. She escaped to Oregon. The information helped explain several things about her mother. Melinda understood a little more why her mother never drove a car, why she had not talked much about her past, and why she looked sad and hurt when Melinda tried to pry.

But, some important pieces were still missing. When did she come into the picture, before or after the accident? Where was her father? Was he killed in the accident? Melinda thought about that possibility so much, she began to think it was true. It would explain why she had never met him, why her mother never wanted to talk about him, and why her mother never wanted to date again. She now could understand why the girl who had lived in Belle Meade in this mansion could also be the grown woman who had lived in Oregon and who was her mother. But, what if her father hadn't died in the accident? She knew that was still a possibility. Until she found out for sure, Melinda decided she couldn't be content to think her father was dead. Somehow, she had to complete the story.

• • •

Two days before school started, Melinda called Glory and asked if she could stay all night with her. She packed a bag and left Charles a note on the kitchen counter.

For as quiet and boring as Charles' house was, Glory's was loud and exciting. Melinda learned how to play euchre, a popular Midwestern card game they told her was a must for her to learn. She sat at the table playing or watching others play most of the day. Jillian came over that evening, and while Glory and Brandy Lee did dishes in the kitchen, Melinda and Jillian were left alone for the first time in over a week.

For several minutes, the two looked everywhere but at each other. Jillian bit her lower lip and studied the pictures on the living wall one by one. Melinda opened a copy of *Ebony* magazine and flipped through the pages. Finally, she said, "Well, school starts in two days."

"Yep," Jillian said.

The telephone rang. Glory entered the room and said, "That was Charles. He said Priscilla is picking you up in the morning to go shopping and register you at Trinity."

"That's just great," Jillian said. "Now, you're going shopping with someone named Priscilla. Ashleigh. Bradley. Priscilla. Where do they come up with these names?"

"Jillian, I don't like this any better than you do. In fact, I'm sure I like it less than you," Melinda said. She tossed the magazine back on the table.

"Then why are you running with Bradley? Why are you shopping with Priscilla? Why are you going to Trinity? Next thing I know, you'll be best friends with Ashleigh." Jillian was standing up now, lifting her fingers high in the air, counting off why she thought Melinda was enjoying the switch to Trinity.

"Jillian," Glory yelled. "Sit down. Melinda lives with her uncle now. She has to do what he says. She has no choice."

Jillian sat down on the couch across from Melinda. "Well, it's not fair. She should be able to go where she wants. She's my friend. I feel like telling Charles a thing or two." She let out a deep breath. "I just hate it, and I'm mad."

"Just because you go to different schools doesn't mean you can't be friends," Brandy Lee said. Melinda hadn't noticed her enter the room. "Look at me and Carole. We were great friends for a long time, and we never went to the same school."

Jillian mumbled something.

"What?" Brandy Lee said.

"Maybe she doesn't want to be friends with me anymore, did you ever think of that?" She looked down at the coffee table.

"I do," Melinda said.

"Well," Jillian still stared at the tabletop. "Maybe, she won't want to be friends anymore after she makes new friends at that school, did you ever think of that?"

"I will," Melinda said.

Jillian slowly looked up and glared at Melinda. "Do you promise?"

"Yes." Melinda said it like she was saying "of course I will."

Jillian smiled and picked up a ceramic apple that was on the end table. She threw it gently at Melinda, who caught it and threw it back.

"Hey, stop that," Glory said. "You could break my apple."

"Grandmama, can we have a slumber party here tonight?" Jillian said. "Can we call Emily and ask her too? Please?" She got down on her knees and cupped her hands together. Glory nodded and Jillian jumped up and hugged her grandmother, almost knocking her down.

"She likes to jump up on people and knock them down," Melinda said with a smile.

Jillian hurried to Melinda on the couch, fell across her lap and hugged her.

"Only people I love," Jillian said.

"Aren't we lucky," Melinda sarcastically responded.

No one mentioned Trinity or switching school the rest of the night. They watched movies, ordered pizza and made a bed across the living room floor. While they were lying in the dark, Melinda told her two friends about her visit to see her grandmother and what she and Charles had said. She told them about her ping-pong thoughts and asked their opinion. Did they think her father died in the accident, or did they think he was still alive?

After much discussion, Emily said she thought her father died in the accident and that's why her mother never talked about him. Jillian had many theories. At first, she said Melinda's mother was so upset about the whole thing that she fell in love with the first man she met on her way to Oregon, maybe someone in St. Louis or Denver. Then she got pregnant, and realized she didn't love the man, so continued on her journey. She didn't ever tell Melinda because she was embarrassed and didn't want to open the whole issue of why she was upset and why she left home. Her next theory was that Melinda's mother really did have a drinking problem because an English professor from Trinity used to have wild parties at his house all the time. He fell in love with Melinda's mom, seduced her and she got pregnant. He paid her to go to Oregon and not tell anyone so he wouldn't lose his job, or worse, go to jail for falling in love with a student.

Melinda picked up her pillow and hit Jillian over the head. "That's disgusting. I don't want to hear any more of your theories."

"Well, how are we going to find out the truth?" Jillian said.

"I've got to find the rest of that diary," Melinda said, tucking her pillow back under her head.

"Maybe we could help," Emily said.

"Yeah," Jillian said, "next weekend, we'll have a sleep over at your house, find the diary and all read it together."

That put an end to the conversation and gave Melinda new hope.

Chapter 17

The next morning, Charles showed up at Glory's instead of Priscilla.

"Priscilla was too damned scared of getting mugged or something. She wouldn't come to pick you up in this neighborhood. She's meeting us at my house," Charles said. He shifted down to second gear as they roared out of Glory's part of town, through the congested street, past the Dairy Queen and into the elite neighborhood of Belle Meade. "I had to pull a few strings to get you into Trinity mid-year. They have a waiting list you just bypassed. Today, I had to pull some more strings to get you an interview and tour of the campus on a Sunday. The interview is just a formality. The principal wants to meet you and show you around before you start tomorrow. He called the special arrangement a 'family favor.' We've put a lot of money into that school over the years."

Melinda had a strange feeling that her life would never be the same again as she looked at Priscilla waving her leather-gloved hand on the front step, acting excited to see them pulling in the driveway. She thought about Glory, Jillian and Emily standing outside Glory's door as she left. Still in their pajamas and bunched together, they waved goodbye. Jillian rubbed her eyes and squinted from the brightness of the outdoors. Melinda forced a smile and waved back.

Now, Priscilla sashayed down the long sidewalk toward them. She stood on her tiptoes and kissed Charles on the cheek. "So happy I can help with this situation, dear," she said.

Priscilla looked at Melinda. "I see the first thing we are going to do is get you a new coat. Oh my, you don't even have buttons on that one." She opened up Melinda's coat and studied her new Shorewood Beach sweatshirt and faded jeans. "You'll need new attire all over. You poor child, those jeans are starting to look like you're expecting a flood. Charles, it's obvious you haven't allowed the child to buy new clothes since she's been here."

"Don't forget that the meeting at Trinity is at 3 p.m. sharp, Priscilla," he said.

"Of course I won't, dear."

In the car, Priscilla was preoccupied with herself. After a close inspection in the rearview mirror, she pulled out a tube of lipstick and began applying it while driving. To her reflection, she puckered her lips and then smacked them together a couple of times. Then, with a finger that was made half an inch longer by a square-tipped nail, she traced the outline of her lips.

"I'm trying out this new pearl lipstick that my Bobbie Brown consultant said would look perfect for my coloring, but I just haven't decided yet," Priscilla glanced over at Melinda with pout lips. "What do you think?"

"Looks fine to me," Melinda said.

Melinda spent the afternoon following Priscilla around the Fashion Mall. Priscilla glided through the racks in the juniors departments, loaded Melinda's arms until she couldn't see over top of the clothes and then stood outside the dressing room door insisting that Melinda model every coat, jacket, blouse and pair of pants. Priscilla also took Melinda to her personal stylist and told the woman to do "something gorgeous" with Melinda's hair and fingernails. After two and a half hours of shopping and an hour at the salon, Melinda said, "Aren't we supposed to be at the school in a few minutes?" She was surprised at how eager she sounded to go to Trinity, but realized it was more appealing than spending another minute shopping with Priscilla.

Melinda felt weighted down as they searched for the car in the vast parking lot. She carried all the bags of clothes that Priscilla said looked gorgeous on her, including her new school uniform of navy blue skirts and white oxford shirts, while Priscilla held one tiny bag of new lipstick and lotions from her Bobbie Brown consultant. Melinda wore a new brown velvet coat with fur trim and a matching pants outfit that Priscilla said was "necessary and appropriate" for a school interview.

• • •

As they drove up the long tree-lined lane to the school, Priscilla pointed out various buildings, talked about her wonderful memories of the school and, all the while, changed her lipstick. When they stopped in front of an old, stately building, Priscilla pulled a pair of tweezers from her cosmetic bag. She leaned as close to the mirror as she could and plucked out eyebrow hairs.

"There," she said. "This is fabulous. I can see so much better in this light. I need to get better lighting in my bathroom." Next, she applied rouge to her cheeks and then turned and dabbed some on Melinda's cheeks.

They got out of the car and Priscilla spread her arms out wide. "Oh, I love this school. It made me what I am today. It taught me that if you have good looks and money, you'll go far."

The principal was waiting for them in his office. The sign above the door said, "Mr. Lawton." He was a serious man who immediately began explaining the history of the school, how her day would be structured and some of the extra-curricular activities available to students. He led them on a tour around the campus and Priscilla commented the entire trip on what had changed and what hadn't. Mr. Lawton seemed bored and ready for the tour to be over.

Melinda studied each building, hallway and room that they entered. Even though it was cold as they walked along the campus sidewalk, Melinda's palms perspired.

In the Main Hall, Mr. Lawton pointed out a picture of her grandmother and grandfather. They were in their graduation gowns and caps. She hadn't even thought about them spending all of their school days here.

Mr. Lawton pointed out that she was actually the fifth generation of the Overstreet family to attend Trinity. It was her great, great grandparents who helped found the school over 100 years ago.

While Priscilla and Mr. Lawton talked in the Kennedy Library, Melinda wandered over to look at another wall of graduation classes. Because the seniors all had matching gowns and caps, Melinda had to look close to distinguish their faces. She knew the year her mother graduated and searched until she found that class. She scanned the faces and in the middle of the third row, almost smack in the middle of the picture, she spotted the familiar wavy sandy-blond hair.

As Melinda stared at the picture, she heard Priscilla say, "Yes, I may come to some of the mother/daughter events with Melinda. I do think that would be charming. I'll have to talk to Charles about it. I am not her aunt yet, of course."

Melinda reached up and touched her mother's face. She swallowed hard and tried to smile at the younger version of the face she'd known so well. She caressed the spot on the glass. She whispered, "You were here. Are you with me now?"

Melinda walked back to the car wondering about her future at Trinity. She felt a strange new bond with the school. After all, her mother, her grandmother, her great grandmother and her great, great grandmother all went there. On the way home, she thought about how that hadn't ever been important before, but now she daydreamed about how she was following a path.

At home, she quickly ran up to her room and changed back into her jeans and Oregon sweatshirt. That night, she felt compelled to write her mother a letter. She pulled a notebook out of the nightstand and wrote:

Dear Mom,

I walked around your old school today. I thought about you. I saw the track where you wanted to run. Tomorrow, I start going to school there, too. Maybe I'll get on the track team and run for both of us. Maybe I'll win, too. Would you like that? Even though you always taught me to be independent and strong, I'm scared now. It feels weird being in all your old places. By the way, you didn't have an English teacher who had wild parties, did you? Stupid question, I know. Forget it. I'm sorry about your car accident. I wish you would have told me about it. I would have understood. Wish I could touch your real face right now. Glory said you are with me all the time. Are you?

I love you,

Mel

• • •

When she finished the letter, Melinda picked up the telephone and called Darcy at home. When no one answered, she called The Loft. A person she didn't know answered and said she'd get Darcy.

"Oh, sweetheart, it is so good to hear your voice," Darcy said. "Is everything okay?"

"Everything's fine," Melinda said. "I just wanted to say hi. I'm starting at that private school tomorrow. You know, the one my mom went to. I saw her picture on the library wall. I was wondering if you could go through her things and see if you can find anything else."

"What do you want me to look for, honey?"

"I don't know. More personal things, maybe some old letters or something. Maybe my birth certificate. Anything like that."

"Okay, Mel. I'll see what else I can find. I need to go now, darling. Are you sure you're all right?"

"Yeah. Thanks Darcy."

• • •

Monday morning, Melinda awoke once again to Charles banging on the door.

"Melinda," he yelled. "We need to leave in 15 minutes. Are you awake?"

"Yeah." Melinda rubbed her eyes and started to sit up. "I'll be right down."

She showered, dressed and hurried to the kitchen with her hair wet. She rummaged through the pantry. She found a Pop Tart and put it in the toaster as Charles whisked through the room with his laptop and briefcase.

"Don't have time to heat it up. You'll have to eat it cold." He walked to the garage and Melinda followed with her cold Pop Tart in hand.

In the car, Charles kept muttering things like "going to have to get up earlier," "can't count on me to wake you up" and "don't know if this will work, might have to find another way for you to get to school." Melinda ate her Pop Tart in tiny bites, trying to catch crumbs in the palm of her other hand. She held the crumbs tightly until she could dump them on the ground.

Charles was on his cell phone as they waited in the long line of cars dropping students off at the front entrance. He kept pulling his sleeve up and looking at his watch and letting out loud grunts. The whole process was new to Melinda, and she watched as each car pulled up, kids got out and then the next car pulled up. When it was almost her turn, Melinda gasped.

"Oh, no," she said.

Charles covered up the phone with his palm. "What? What is it?"

"No one else has a uniform on. I thought we had to wear uniforms. Priscilla said this was the school uniform."

"Looks like the school uniform to me," Charles said, glancing down at her blue skirt and white shirt.

"Maybe things have changed since you went here."

"It's not that big of a deal. So what? Even if it's not the uniform, it's a nice outfit."

"Kids my age don't normally wear something like this, unless they have too. I feel like an idiot." She got out of the car at the main entrance and almost shut the door. "Oh, thanks for the ride."

Melinda walked to the principal's office with her head down the whole way. She was sure everyone was looking at her. She was new and she was the only one dressed in a uniform. She collected her classroom list and stack of textbooks, found her locker and put her coat and extra books in it. Her first class was biology and she groaned to herself as she approached the door. Ashleigh, Brad and some other students were standing near the door. Ashleigh had on a pair of bell-bottom jeans and a stylish shirt. She giggled as Melinda passed.

"So sorry no one told you we don't wear uniforms on the first day back to school," Ashleigh said in a whining voice. "Mr. Overstreet probably forgot. It's been so long since he went here." She looked around like she expected someone else to add comments about Melinda's dress. Melinda tried to smile as she walked by hugging her books close to her chest.

"What was that all about?" Brad said to Ashleigh just as Melinda passed the group. "Sometimes I don't get you, Ashleigh." He left the group and walked around the corner. Ashleigh huffed and then followed Melinda into the classroom.

Melinda stood still just inside the door for a minute, not knowing which seat she should take. The teacher walked in and introduced himself as Mr. Upton and then introduced Melinda to the class. He told her she could take the empty seat near the window. Melinda started across the room, and then froze when she realized it was right in front of Ashleigh.

Melinda got the feeling that Ashleigh was staring at the back of her head the entire class. At one point, Ashleigh scooted Melinda's chair a few inches into the aisle with her foot. Melinda scooted it back and tried to convince herself that it was an accident, and that Ashleigh did not do that on purpose. Mr. Upton asked Melinda a question about microorganisms. Melinda said she didn't know the answer and that she hadn't gotten that far into biology at her old schools. Ashleigh raised her hand and proudly answered the question. After class, Mr. Upton suggested that Melinda try to catch up with the rest of the class. At her locker, she changed books and whispered, "Please, let the rest of the day go better than that."

During lunchtime, Melinda grabbed a few items from the buffet line, sat at the end of one table and pretended to read her history book. After her morning classes, she'd learned she was behind in all the subjects.

She heard a group of girls talking at the next table.

"We're going to Aspen next month," one girl said.

"My family prefers the Swiss Alps," another one said.

"Well, we get to go to Bora Bora for spring break," a third one said. "I already bought my suit and Wesley said I look sexy in it." The girls all giggled. Melinda had never heard students talking about such elaborate family vacations.

After lunch, she was relieved when she walked into music class. How could she be behind in this class? Her music teacher, Mrs. Doyle, was a short, middle-aged woman who didn't waste time or words. They were singing within five minutes of the bell. When the teacher wasn't playing the piano, she walked around listening to the students sing. At the end of class, she encouraged them to participate in the Spring Sing. A few members of the choir would be selected to do solos at the concert. Practices would start after school next month.

The last class of the day was gym and as Melinda entered the locker room she heard Ashleigh's voice, and groaned. Not again.

Melinda found a private area to change. Ashleigh and her friends were loud.

"Do you think I'm getting fat?" Ashleigh asked.

"Oh, please," a girl answered. "You're a bone. I think you are obsessed with your weight."

"Aren't we all?" Ashleigh said. "My mom says I better watch my weight. My sister gained 10 pounds when she started college. My mom will not let her hear the end of that. Do you think my stomach is sticking out more?"

A whistle blew and everyone hurried toward the gymnasium. Melinda finished tying the shoestring on her new tennis shoes and followed the group. The girls all stood on the line bordering the basketball court. They faced Mrs. Cox, the physical education teacher, who stood in the middle of the room. She took roll call and then told everyone to do ten laps around the gym. Melinda stayed toward the back of the line and jogged slowly. She didn't want to get near Ashleigh and her friends. After a few laps, Melinda noticed Ashleigh trying to catch her from behind. The faster Ashleigh ran, the faster Melinda did. She started passing most of the class to maintain the distance between them. Everyone watched. Mrs. Cox yelled "Nine" as Ashleigh passed her. From half way across the room, Melinda thought, only one more lap. Ashleigh ran harder. Melinda ran harder. Ashleigh rounded the corner where Mrs. Cox was and the teacher yelled "Ten." Melinda slowed down and then finished a few seconds later. The teacher looked at her stopwatch as Melinda passed her. The rest of the class had at least two more laps to go. Ashleigh and Melinda were still breathing hard when Mrs. Cox told them to find a seat on the bleachers. They sat at opposite ends.

After several minutes, everyone else joined them on the bleachers except one short, pigeon-toed girl with short, red hair. Melinda heard Ashleigh say something and then the girls around her giggled. Melinda felt sorry for the girl out on the floor as Mrs. Cox said, "One more." When she was done, the girl sat in front of Melinda.

"Spring track season starts in just a few weeks," Mrs. Cox said with her clipboard tucked under her arm. "I want Trinity to win the spring invitational. We were close in the fall. With a little extra effort, we can win. We will win. We have three strong finishers in each category, except cross-country. But, after what I saw just a few minutes ago, I think we will have at least two contenders this season." She looked at Melinda and smiled.

"Today, we work on strength building," Mrs. Cox continued.

Many of the girls groaned.

"To the weight room." Mrs. Cox turned around and waved her arm high in the air. "Follow me."

While lifting weights, Melinda managed to stay far away from Ashleigh. She noticed one of Ashleigh's friends cut in front of the pigeon-toed girl two times while waiting for different machines. In the locker room, Melinda stayed to herself. The bell rang for school dismissal just as she finished changing back into her uniform.

Ashleigh was waiting outside the locker room and walked next to Melinda. "Don't think you are going to be my backup on the track team," she said softly. "My mom is president of the PTA, and the athletic director is my uncle. A new rule is being written this week. Only students who start at the beginning of the school year can be on the track team. Sorry."

While Melinda stood in the wake of Ashleigh's remarks, she realized she didn't know how she was getting home. Charles hadn't mentioned it this morning. She didn't expect he would leave his downtown office to pick her up from school in the middle of the day. She took her time at the locker and by the time she got outside, most of the cars picking up students were gone. Just a few other students sat on the steps. Maybe her uncle would come, or maybe he would send someone to pick her up. She waited until the last student was gone and then went to the office and called Glory.

Outside, she placed the heavy backpack beside her and pulled her old coat tighter around her body. Who cared if the buttons were gone? She didn't. As the sky clouded up and the temperature dropped, she thought maybe she should have worn the new fur-lined coat after all. At least, she would be warmer now. She looked down at her worn nylon coat and ran her hand down the sleeve. Then, she sat on her hands to try to warm them. She lowered her chin and nestled it in the top of her coat. Had it been a year ago already that she bought this coat?

"Hey, I got the tax check in the mail today, Mel," her mother had said. "We're not rich, but we do have a little extra loot! Should we fly to Paris for the weekend or buy new coats and splurge on a pizza with the works?

Melinda laughed. Her mother flipped a coin.

"Coats and pizza win. But wait, I'm having a brainstorm. Let me look at the size of that check again." Her mother peeped inside the envelope. "Yes, it's big enough. Let's go to Portland for the weekend. We'll shop at our favorite Salvation Army. Stay at a hotel and eat at the restaurant of your choice."

Her mother grabbed her hands and they danced around the kitchen floor. "It's going to be a girls' weekend," she sang.

"Good thing you don't sing for a living," Melinda said. "We'd be poor."

"You know a music teacher actually asked me to just mouth the words once?" her mother said. "Can you believe that?"

Melinda nodded and they both laughed.

"You're lucky. No one will ever say that to you," her mother said.

Mack was attending a hardware store convention in Portland and they hitched a ride with him for the weekend. He dropped them off in the downtown market area on Saturday and picked them back up Sunday afternoon. They each got new coats and picked out one other piece of clothing. Her mother bought a new pair of jeans and Melinda chose the blue sweater that her mother had wanted her to wear the night she died. They stayed in a tall, old hotel downtown that looked out over the river.

They could see Mt. Hood in the distance. They swam in the pool and ate at a Chinese restaurant in Chinatown.

On the way home, Mack and her mother sang James Taylor songs in the front seat. Melinda wrapped her coat around her. "I feel like a princess in my new coat and this new car." Mack and her mother smiled at each other and Melinda pretended they were a family.

Glory pulled up then and Melinda threw her backpack over her shoulder and ran toward the car.

Chapter 18

Glory parked and followed Melinda into the house. They both went straight to the kitchen. "How about some soup and a grilled cheese sandwich?" Glory opened a cabinet. "You just sit and relax."

"Sounds good to me," Melinda said. She pulled out a chair and slouched down.

"So how was the first day?" Glory asked.

"Not so good."

"Want to talk about it?"

"No. Yes. First, I was the only one to wear a uniform. No one told me that you don't have to wear a uniform the first day back from Christmas break."

"Oh, brother." Glory flipped the grilled cheese sandwiches over while Melinda watched her from the table.

"I sat by myself at lunch. Almost every teacher told me I needed to do extra work at home to catch up with the rest of the class."

"That's ridiculous. How do they expect you do catch up and keep doing the homework they give you?"

"See what I mean? It was a bad day, and it gets worse."

"No!" Glory empathized while stirring the soup.

"Yes. Ashleigh sits behind me in biology and I think she pushed my chair out in the aisle on purpose."

"That little bugger." Glory brought two plates to the table and then went back to ladle two bowls of soup.

"She's also in my gym class. All the eighth graders are together. After we ran, Mrs. Cox, who is the gym teacher and girls' track coach, said I would be a good addition to the team or something like that."

"*That* was a good thing."

"Yeah," Melinda took a big bite of her sandwich. "That was good, but after gym Ashleigh said that there was a new rule that her PTA president mom made that said only students who started in the fall could be on the track team."

"No way." Glory brought the soup bowls to the table and sat down. "I think Charles could do something about that.

"No, please don't mention it to him. I don't even care anyway. I would have to see her at every practice, and I'd rather just run on my own around here."

Melinda heard the garage door open. Charles grunted "hello" as he swept through the room.

"Excuse me," Glory said to Melinda as she followed Charles down the hall. At first, Melinda couldn't make out their words and wasn't concerned, but after she heard Charles say loudly, "I didn't plan on raising a teenage girl," she perked up. Glory's voice grew louder too.

"Charles Overstreet. We don't plan for a lot of things in life. She didn't plan for her mother to die. She didn't plan to move to a strange town and be surrounded with strange people. Mercy. Do you ever think of anyone but yourself?"

Charles hissed something that Melinda couldn't hear. She sipped her soup and felt like an eavesdropper, but the only other choice was to walk past them to her room. Sitting quietly seemed the better option.

"Don't shush me, Charles. How did you think she was supposed to get home today?" Charles mumbled again. "You forgot! Well, where does that leave her? You wanted her in that school. I had her in a school with bus service. It's your doin' and your responsibility. Like it or not, Charles, you have new responsibilities. And you better work on it. You have a beautiful, growing young lady in there who needs you."

Glory marched back into the kitchen and dropped down in her chair. "Sorry you had to hear that," she said. "Sometimes I get so angry."

Melinda watched Glory slouch down in the chair. The old woman's energy seemed to disappear and for the first time, Melinda noticed how old Glory really was. Her whole body drooped. She took a deep breath and closed her eyes. Melinda waited for a minute, but Glory didn't open her eyes.

"Glory," she said cautiously. Glory slowly opened her eyes and smiled sweetly.

"Yes, dear."

"I thought you'd fallen asleep for a second."

"No, just resting. I've been a little under the weather lately," Glory said. "Or, maybe I'm just getting old. I'll be 78 this year. I chased the twins around half the day and cleaned their house the other half. Just can't keep up like I used to. I should get home."

"I need to do homework anyway," commented Melinda. They stood up from the table, put the dishes in the dishwasher and walked toward the front door.

"Keep your chin up, sweetie," Glory said putting her hand under Melinda's chin. "You'll make friends at Trinity soon. You are one special lady. Show 'em what you're made of. You're better than all of them put together. You got that, girl?"

Melinda smiled and gave Glory a big hug. "Thanks for everything."

• • •

From then on, Melinda set the alarm and was finished eating breakfast before Charles even entered the kitchen. He drove her to school each day, but they talked very little. He always made at least one telephone call during their trip. He arranged for Priscilla or Glory to pick her up most days. Occasionally, she rode home with strangers, parents of other students who Charles had called and asked to pick her up. He knew more Trinity parents than Melinda would have guessed. At first, she wondered why she didn't ever ride home with Brad and

Mrs. Rutherford, and then figured out that he had track practice after school. In the evenings, she worked hard to catch up in all of her classes. Many nights, she fell asleep with the light on and an open book next to her. After a few weeks, she went from getting some of the worst grades to some of the best, except in biology, which was a difficult subject for her.

Ashleigh continued to do childish things at school. She scooted Melinda's chair into the aisle just enough so that nobody else would notice except Melinda. When she passed out papers, she accidentally dropped Melinda's on the floor on the other side of her desk so that Melinda had to pick them up. After not getting a response from Melinda, Ashleigh stopped bugging her.

Track practice started, but Mrs. Cox never mentioned Melinda being on the team again. Neither did Melinda.

One day, when the physical education class was running around the gym, the pigeon-toed girl, whose name was Alita, fell. Ashleigh and her friends snickered, but Melinda stopped to see if she was okay. Her knee had hit the floor hard. Melinda helped her up, put Alita's arm over her shoulder and supported her as the two walked to the bleachers.

The next day at lunch, Alita asked if she could sit with Melinda.

"Thanks again for yesterday," Alita said. She seemed embarrassed and wouldn't look Melinda in the eyes.

"How's your knee today?" Melinda asked.

"It's okay. I'm used to falling. I've had scars on my knees most of my life. I bet you've never fallen. You're such a great runner."

"Thanks."

"Why aren't you on the track team? I'd love to see you beat Ashleigh."

"Join the crowd," Melinda said.

"What?"

"I've had other people tell me they want me to beat Ashleigh. I just decided to concentrate on classes this year."

"If you need any help in biology, I'm pretty good at it," Alita said.

"I'll take you up on that offer. I do need the help."

Alita looked up and smiled at Melinda. "Okay," she said.

The sleepover with Jillian and Emily kept being postponed weekend after weekend. One weekend, Melinda had to go to Charles' lake house in Southwest Michigan to watch the twins while her uncle and Priscilla went to dinner and a play in the small resort town. The next couple of weekends, Emily or Jillian had other plans. When they finally got together, it was just for the afternoon. They looked briefly for the diary without success and then just lay around in Melinda's room and talked. Melinda had invited Alita and was pleased when Jillian and Emily liked her too.

Jillian and Emily talked about track practice and the approaching season with excitement. When Melinda didn't say much about her practice, they encouraged her by saying that she'd be sure to beat Ashleigh at the spring invitational this time. Melinda felt Alita looking at her and knew she was wondering why she didn't tell her friends that she wasn't even on the track team. Finally, Melinda broke down and told them.

"What?" Jillian and Emily said at the same time.

"I'm really behind in classes and I needed to focus on that," Melinda said.

"Something's not right," Jillian said. "You're still running aren't you? I know you wouldn't stop running."

"Just on the weekends," Melinda said.

"With Brad?" Jillian said.

Melinda didn't answer.

"You're not telling me everything, Melinda Overstreet," Jillian said. "I know you and you're not telling me something."

"Ashleigh said I can't be on the team because I'm new to the school. Her mom makes the rules."

"I'm gonna march right over to their house tonight and tell them they can't do that," Jillian said. "I bet that's against the law or something. Charles would know. I'm going to ask him." She walked toward the door and flung it open.

"He's not home," Melinda said.

"I bet if you asked him, he'd tell you it's against the law," Jillian persisted. "Girl, you gotta be on that team. You gotta stand up to that witch. I always knew she was low, but this is *really* low. Don't let her get away with it."

After the girls left, Melinda thought about standing up to Ashleigh and her mom and telling them they didn't have a right to exclude her from the team. Charles had said that the Overstreets were important to the school. If she told the principal, she probably could get on the team. But, on the other hand, she was new and she didn't want to cause a commotion. When Alita brought it up again the next week at school, Melinda explained why she didn't want to do anything about it, and Alita said she understood.

One day after lunch, as Melinda and Alita entered the bathroom, they heard gagging coming from one of the stalls. They stopped talking and exchanged curious looks. Melinda held one finger to her mouth. After another gag and the sound of someone throwing up, the girls slowly backed up and left the bathroom. In the hall, they wrinkled their noses.

"That was gross," Melinda said.

"She's done it for a long time," Alita said.

"What do you mean? Who?"

"Ashleigh."

"You mean she really does it on purpose? Jillian guessed it. She said everyone here does it."

Alita laughed. "Not everyone. She's the only one I know who does it. A lot of people know she does, but I think they all just ignore it."

"I almost feel sorry for her," Melinda said.

"Not me. She's too mean to feel sorry for."

That night Melinda looked up eating disorders on the Internet and found the definition of bulimia. She was surprised to discover that people who have this can collapse and even die. When she mentioned Ashleigh's problem to Jillian, her friend said, "It couldn't happen to a nicer person."

• • •

In February, getting a ride home from school got worse. Charles seemed to have forgotten Glory's lecture. Melinda didn't call Glory because she didn't want to upset her anymore. Each time she'd visited her old friend over the past weeks, she thought Glory looked more tired. When asked about it, Glory said she "had a bug she couldn't get rid of." When Melinda called Charles at work, he sent a taxi to pick her up. She was glad no other students were around when it arrived. She couldn't wait to tell Darcy she'd taken her first taxi ride, though, it was from school to home, nothing as exciting as Darcy had imagined.

Alita came over and helped Melinda with biology. When she mentioned the taxi ride, Alita said, "You can start riding home with me. My mom wouldn't mind at all." Melinda felt relieved and wished she had mentioned the problem to Alita long ago.

• • •

At least once each weekend, she did run with Brad. It was one of the highlights of her week. One morning, it had snowed over six inches and Melinda was disappointed. She didn't think they would be able to run, but Brad showed up at the door with "ice joggers," lightweight rubber pieces with spikes that provided traction in the snow. They pulled the ice joggers onto the bottom of their shoes and ran through the snow-covered streets.

The ground was a shimmering white blanket. After running for 20 minutes, they stopped in the park to look around at the trees. Everything sparkled. Even the smallest twigs glistened in the sunlight. Now, she knew the meaning of a "winter wonderland." Melinda told Brad running in the snow reminded her of running on the sand at home, but the snow was even more beautiful.

"I think running in sand would be harder," Brad said.

"That's how I started. We were near the beach so our yard didn't have much dirt, mostly just sand. When I was really young, like four or five, I always wanted to race my mom from the front of the house to the back of the house. We'd do that, then turn around and race back to the front. As I got older, we'd run all the way around the house."

Brad laughed. "Did you ever win?"

"I always just barely beat her. Now, it sounds crazy, but I never doubted that I really won. Well, until I was about ten or eleven, then I started saying, 'You're not trying.'"

"Then what happened?"

"We started running further. We'd race down our street. Then, we'd race from the water's edge to our house. Then, we'd race from a mile away, then two miles. You get the picture. We'd always start by saying, 'Race you home!'"

"But did she still let you win after you complained?"

"No. I didn't win for years, not until last year."

"Did she let you?"

"No. I really won," Melinda said. She grinned at Brad and took off running.

"Hey, wait!"

"Race you home!" Melinda yelled over her shoulder.

"You caught me off guard. The road's too slippery to run this hard. Melinda, I just almost fell for real."

Melinda laughed and ran as hard as she could. He caught up to her a few houses from their's. When she thought he was about to pass her, she playfully shoved him off the road. He stumbled and ran to catch up again.

When they got to their yards, he said, "Now I know how you started winning." They laughed and started walking in opposite directions to their houses. "Sorry to hear about you not being able to be on the track team. I could have my dad talk to your uncle," Brad yelled from across the street. "Ashleigh told me what you told the coach."

Melinda stopped and turned around to face him. "What was that?"

"You know." Brad said. "That Charles said you couldn't be on the team, just like your grandmother told your mom."

Melinda frowned. "You know, she is really starting to make me angry. She lied, Brad. I did not say that to the coach. She told me I could not be on the team because her mom made a rule about new students not being allowed to join the team. Urgh!" Melinda screamed in frustration and then marched into the house.

• • •

At school a few days later, the principal knocked on the door, entered biology class and then asked Melinda and Ashleigh to follow him to the office. Melinda had never been called to the principal's office and was nervous as they walked down the hall. Mr. Lawton looked unconcerned and only talked about the weather.

When they entered his office, a man who had been sitting with his back to them, stood up and turned around. Melinda was surprised to see Mr. Rutherford. She looked around to see if Brad was also in the room, but he was not. Mr. Rutherford said hello and motioned for her to sit near him.

Mrs. Josten walked in the room with her fingers wrapped around a cup of coffee. She looked angry and didn't greet anyone. She and Ashleigh sat in the chairs facing Melinda and Mr. Rutherford.

"Mr. Rutherford has brought something to my attention." Mr. Lawton said to Melinda. "Apparently, there has been a misunderstanding."

He was interrupted by a knock on the door.

"Come in," he said. Mrs. Cox, the running coach, entered. "Please take my seat. I'll pull up another chair." As he did, he continued talking. "Where was I? Oh, yes, it seems there has been some sort of misunderstanding." He looked at Mrs. Josten and Ashleigh. "Apparently, Ashleigh told Mrs. Cox that Melinda could not participate in track because of her uncle. We contacted Charles and he said that was not the case. Mr. Rutherford and his son, Brad, are under the impression that Melinda is not being allowed to participate on the track team this year because she is new." He shifted in his seat and looked toward Mrs. Cox. "Mrs. Cox, I was unaware of this rule. Can you explain, please?"

Mrs. Cox looked surprised. She turned toward Mrs. Josten, who gave her a curt smile and then looked down at her coffee mug. Ashleigh also stared at her mother's cup. Melinda watched Mrs. Josten. Her face appeared tight and her dark red lipstick was smudged in the v of her upper lip. Her large, gold earrings matched her necklace.

"I'd love to have Melinda on the cross-country team, Mr. Lawton," Mrs. Cox said. "You're right. I think there has been a big misunderstanding."

Melinda felt Mr. Rutherford look at her.

"Melinda, would you like to be on Trinity's cross-country team?" Mr. Rutherford asked in a soft voice.

Everyone was looking at Melinda, except Mrs. Josten, who was peering out the window and sipping her coffee, and Ashleigh, who hadn't raised her head the entire meeting.

Melinda said, "Yes, I would."

Mr. Lawton stood up first and then everyone followed him to the door. Mrs. Josten and Ashleigh never looked up or said a word. They tramped down the hall, the younger one following behind the older one. Mr. Rutherford walked with Melinda all the way back to her locker. "Let me know if you need anything else, okay?"

"Okay. Thanks."

• • •

At lunch, Melinda told Alita about her visit to the office.

"All right," Alita cheered. "That's great. That'll show them. Now, I can't wait until the day you beat Ashleigh at that track meet." Alita raised her hand into the air and Melinda gave her a high five. Wait. What about Spring

Sing practice? It starts tonight and it's after school. We were going to go together."

"I don't know."

In music, Melinda mentioned the conflict to Mrs. Doyle. "I'll talk to Mrs. Cox, and we'll see what we can work out."

During gym, Mrs. Cox announced that Melinda was joining the track team and would participate in the invitational. Several girls cheered, Alita the loudest. Ashleigh was much more quiet than normal. She didn't laugh when Alita missed the soccer ball, and she didn't try to keep the ball away from Melinda like she usually did. She moped back to the locker room by herself.

After gym, Mrs. Cox said the plan was for Melinda to run with the boys' team on the days she had Spring Sing practice. The boys did weight training first and started running about the time choir practice was over. She asked if Melinda minded that, and she said no. To herself, she thought it would be better. She wouldn't have to be around Ashleigh.

Melinda was glad to be running again. After a couple of practices, the boys accepted her and were surprised how well she was able to keep up. She set her sights on beating Ashleigh. She wanted to win for Alita, Jillian, and most of all, her mother. It became one of the biggest goals of her life.

Chapter 19

Melinda turned the pages on her calendar so quickly that she was surprised one day to see that over two months had flown by since she joined Trinity's cross-country team. She had been busy running, practicing for the Spring Sing, keeping up with her class work and spending any free time with her friends and Glory. Now, it was May and the Spring All City Invitational and the Spring Sing were just a few weeks away. Her excitement about the month also included graduating from eighth grade and Darcy's visit.

"Glory, I can't believe everything that's happening this month," Melinda said to Glory the first week of May. She listed everything to the older woman who just smiled in return. Melinda in turn watched Glory closely. "I don't think you're getting any better, Glory. Have you been to a doctor?"

Glory chuckled. "No, I haven't. You spend too much time worrying about me. You got your own things to think about."

"Oh, no," Melinda exclaimed. "I didn't know it was so late! I'm supposed to be watching the twins tonight."

Melinda rode home on her mother's old bicycle. She'd found it a few weeks ago and had stopped relying on other people for rides. It was a Motobecane, an expensive French bike that only took a few minor repairs to get back in working order.

The twins ran to greet Melinda as soon as she entered the house. Charles and Priscilla were all dressed up and left within a few minutes.

Jake suggested they play cops and robbers. He told Sam to be the bad guy.

"I don't want to be the bad guy," Sam said. "They always lose."

"I'll give you this ransom note if you're the bad guy." Jake pulled a crumpled piece of paper from his jeans' pocket. "You can use it to kidnap Linda. It says Daddy has to pay $500 million dollars to get her back."

Melinda laughed. "What if he doesn't want to pay that much to get me back?"

"Why wouldn't he?" Sam asked.

"He will." Jake said.

Sam pretended to tie Melinda to a chair in his room. While Melinda sat on the floor against the chair, Sam said he was going to tell his daddy how much he needed to pay to get Melinda back. As he ran out the door, the piece of paper fell from his pocket.

Melinda reached down to pick it up. A handwritten note said, "I think I've totally messed up my life this time." Most of the page was torn off. Melinda looked at it for a minute before recognizing the yellowed paper and script. It was from her mother's diary. She quickly ran downstairs to find the boys.

"Where in the world did you guys get this?" She waved the paper in her hand. "Where is the rest of the book?" She was talking louder than normal, and the boys looked frightened. "You are not in trouble. This is from my mom's diary. I've been looking all over for it. Can you tell me where the rest of it is?"

They looked at each other.

"I don't know," Sam said. "Jake had it."

"Sam gave it to me."

"Okay, boys. Let's sit down. Think. Where might you have gotten this?"

"Maybe in your room," Sam said.

"I don't think so. I've cleaned my room many times in the past months looking for it. Was it in your room?"

"Maybe."

"Yeah. Maybe."

The threesome went back to the boys' room and looked all over for the rest of the book. Finally, Melinda sat on the bed, shoulders slumped. Her mother's diary was probably scattered in a hundred pieces. She would never be able to read it.

"Are you sad?" Sam said snuggling next to Melinda. Jake climbed on the other side of her and leaned his head against her body.

"It's okay, guys. It was just sort of important to me."

Suddenly, Sam straightened up. He looked across Melinda to Jake. "Maybe, it's in the secret passageway, Jake." Jake's eyes got wide, he jumped off the bed and the two ran to Melinda's room.

"Where are you going?"

They got on their hands and knees and crawled through the closet. Melinda followed them. In back of the long, skinny closet behind some old clothes, they moved a piece of painted wood and went through a small, square hole cut in the wall.

"Guys, I can't see anything. Are you sure it's safe in here? What if we fall through a hole?" Melinda asked. She stopped moving, but heard the boys still scurrying across the wooden-planked floor. She sneezed. "It's so dusty in here. Let's go, boys. Nothing's in here but lots of dirt and maybe a bat or two."

"Wait, Linda. We have hidden flashlights." Just then, two round beams of light appeared, one right in Melinda's eyes.

"Don't shine it in anyone's face, please," Melinda instructed. "May I use one of those?"

One of the twins handed her a flashlight and she searched the dark crawlspace. The walls were covered with photographs of a handsome young man with black hair, blue eyes and a cleft chin just like Melinda's. Some of the pictures were taken close up, some farther away and some with a musical band in the background. In almost all of the photos the man was singing. Melinda slowly shined the flashlight around the entire secret room. She stopped on a picture of her mother with her arm around the young man. Her mother and the man were smiling at each other. The photo was signed, "To Carole. With Love. Johnny."

"Is this what you were looking for?" Sam said holding out the gold book.

"Yes!" Melinda took the book in her hand and held it to her chest. "Thanks so much."

"Are you happy again?" Jake said.

Melinda laughed. "Yes, I am.

"Now, let's go play cops and robbers again," Sam said. "You have to get back by that chair. The good guy, that's Jake, is going to try to rescue you."

"Why don't we play 'read the secret diary'?" Melinda suggested as she followed the boys back through the closet.

"No, that's boring," Jake said. "We found it for you. Now, you have to play with us."

Melinda knew her efforts to talk two five-year-olds into letting her read her mother's diary were useless. She gave in and started toward her ransom spot. Sam grabbed at the diary. "Ransom note," he said.

"Wait. I have a better ransom note." She tore a piece of paper out of one of her school notebooks and wrote the ransom note as they described it earlier. "Here, it says exactly what you wanted it to. Boys, promise me you won't ever touch these diary pages again. Otherwise, I'll be very sad again."

"Promise. Now, let's play."

Melinda was totally worn out by the time Charles got home that night. The twins had been so wound up she couldn't get them to sleep until after 11 p.m. When she finally made it back to her room and her mother's diary, she decided to gather it all up in a stack and read it tomorrow.

In the morning, she called Jillian to ask her to come over and read it with her.

Brandy Lee dropped Jillian off at the door, and said, "Good luck, girls. Let me know what you find out. And don't believe everything you read about me. Maybe I should stay and help you."

"No," both girls said at the same time.

They ran up the stairs to Melinda's room and shut the door behind them.

"Your boyfriend was stretching out in his yard, getting ready to go running," Jillian said. "I'm surprised you're not going, too."

"He's not my boyfriend, and I told him we had something important to do this morning. You said you were going to give me a break about Brad since he helped me get on the cross-country team, remember?"

"I remember," Jillian said. "But I still can't imagine him actually doing something nice. Hey, I want to see the secret room with all the pictures first."

"Okay, follow me."

Inside the small room, Jillian said, "Wow, this guy's got to be your dad. Hey, Melinda, look at this one. It has his whole name, Johnny Ventura and the Bad Fellows Band. We can find him for sure now."

"Let's get out of here and start with the diary," Melinda said. "I've waited long enough."

Back in her room, Melinda opened a thin drawer in the middle of the desk and pulled out a tiny key. Then, she used the key to open the big drawer on the side of the old desk. Jillian raised her eyebrows at Melinda.

"I'm not taking any chances this time." She gently lifted out the book. "I thought we could just start from the beginning and see if anything sounds interesting." The girls plopped down on the bed and began reading.

They flipped through several pages quickly.

"These are boring, things about the weather, projects in school," Jillian said. "If you want to read the boring stuff, you can read it later. I just want the good stuff. Wait, this one's kind of good."

Jillian began to read out loud. *Diary, you've been lost for a long time.*

"You can say that again," Jillian said, smiling at Melinda.

"Keep going," Melinda said.

At the beginning of the year, I told my mother I was not going to dance lessons anymore. At first she wouldn't let me quit, but after I refused to try during the lessons, Mrs. Wagner told her she was wasting her money. She was furious. They both were. Dad didn't really care. He only cares about work, what's for dinner and reading the newspaper. Mother said I'd never run on a cross-country team ever, not one single year in high school. We had a big fight, and are not speaking now. I'm thinking about running away. Why can't I do what I want to do? Why do I always have to do what she wants me to?

"Oooweee. You're mama was a handful, sounds like to me."

Melinda had to agree with Jillian. "Listen to this. This must have been when she became a vegetarian," she said.

Meat is disgusting. I hate going to the butcher with mother. You know he has the nerve to put pictures of deer and moose and baby calves right in his store. While we were there today, I decided I am going to be a vegetarian. I've been thinking about it for a while. Those poor creatures are helpless. Meat is bad for you anyway. Mother, of course, thinks it's just a phase I'm going through and that it won't last long. I'll prove her wrong.

"She did have quite an attitude." Jillian turned the page. "Here's something about a boy."

Mark and I played basketball today. Of course, he is much better than me. He's also much older. He's one of the best on the team at high school. He may even get to play in college.

"Who's Mark?" Jillian said.

"Brad's dad. He was friends with Charles and my mother.

Jillian turned another page.

"Wait. Wait. Wait. I found something with my mama's name."

Brandy Lee met a guy named Jeff Jones about a month ago, since then I never see her anymore. They are always going to each other's houses and watching television she says. Wink. Wink.

"Hey, wait a minute. What does she think they are doing? That ain't right to say that about your best friend," Jillian said, sounding indignant. She sat up in the bed and kept reading.

They are working together at Dairy Queen. He said he's going to own the place someday. When he says that, she looks at him all googly-eyed.

"Well, he wasn't far off," Jillian said, smiling.

She's still my best friend even though we don't see each other much. And, I still can't stand most of the girls at my school. Glory's on her way over to take me to driver's education. She will be the only one who misses me when I get out of this town someday.

For the next several minutes, the girls flipped through pages.

"This book must be 100 pages," Jillian said. "I can't believe she wrote so much." Then she rolled over on her back and stretched out.

"Here's another guy's name." Melinda said.

"What's it say?"

Yesterday, I got burned by Rob Z. I was beginning to like him, but last night Brandy Lee and I saw him strolling along at the mall holding hands with another girl. Boy, do I feel like a fool. I'm not going out with anyone else for a long time.

Brandy Lee said she thinks she's in love, and it doesn't bother her one bit if Jeff is white. I'm getting used to him always being around. He's pretty cool I guess.

Jillian smiled at Melinda. "I think so too," she said. "I don't think Rob Z. is your dad though. He dumped her for another chick."

"You never know. I'm writing it down anyway. Maybe they got back together later. *This* is kind of interesting."

I will be so glad to get out of here. I want to move to the mountains or someplace where there are wide-open spaces, somewhere near a beach where I can feel the wind in my hair, where I can run without traffic lights every couple of feet. Maybe South Carolina or Oregon. I've heard they are both beautiful. I tie-dyed a bunch of my shirts and pants last week. Mother about died. I started wearing wire-rimmed glasses just to look like John Lennon. I bought a Jimi Hendrix tape. I've been running everyday, and I love it!

Melinda rolled over on the bed and stared up at the yellow canopy for a long time. Her mother thought about moving far away before the accident. It wasn't such a last minute thought like Charles had said. She always wanted to live in Oregon. It may not have been "escaping" the accident. In the diary, her mother sounded young, like Melinda herself. It was weird to think of her mother being her age, being immature, being a teenager.

Jillian stretched her arms out to the side. "I'm thirsty. Can we take a break and get something to drink?"

"Sure."

Downstairs, Melinda continued to read through the pages. Jillian finished her drink and then turned on the television. Melinda narrowed her eyes at her.

"I'm tired of reading. You tell me if you find anything else." Jillian slouched down on the couch and pointed the remote toward the screen.

Melinda continued to read.

We have pen pals through school. Mine is a guy named Antonio Ventura. He's from Southern Italy.

"Jill, I found a guy with the last name Ventura like the singer in the pictures, but he has a different first name" Melinda said. Jillian didn't seem to hear her so Melinda kept reading.

We've been writing for over three months now. He sent me a picture. He's pretty cute. He said he thinks I'm cute too. For Christmas, we decided to call each other. It was weird talking to somewhere so far away. His English wasn't very good. He kept getting the words mixed up, and couldn't figure out what I was saying most of the time. He said he would love to go to "universitia" in Chicago. At first, I tried to tell him to go somewhere else, but he didn't understand, so I said, "Yeah, Chicago's great."

"My mom had a pen pal from Italy," Melinda said. Jillian grunted, but continued to watch the show. "I guess that show is more interesting."

"Um? What?"

"Nothing." Melinda flipped through several pages looking for Antonio's name.

Antonio wrote yesterday saying he has a brother in a rock band in Chicago. His band is playing this weekend, not far from here. Brandy Lee has to work, so I'm going with Sheila from algebra class.

Melinda scanned the pages until she found Antonio's name again.

Antonio's brother was awesome. Sheila and I melted every time he opened his mouth to sing. He has long, black hair and green eyes. (I saw them up close after the concert. I told the security guy I was a friend of the family, and his brother Antonio wanted me to deliver a message.) His name is Johnny. I couldn't hardly speak when we met him. He is such a hunk. When we were leaving, he invited us back next week for another concert. He said we could sit in the front row. We're going for sure!

Melinda quickly turned the pages for more information.

I just got an "urgent" letter from Antonio. He said he wished I wasn't infatuated with his brother and to stay away from him. He said Johnny likes all girls. He said I will get hurt. The concert is tonight and I can't wait! I'm not worried about getting hurt.

Melinda flipped to the backside. She was so excited she couldn't keep her hand from trembling and the paper from jiggling.

I went to the concert. Afterwards, Johnny took me and Sheila to a restaurant. He ordered a beer and let me sip it too. He said not to pay attention to what Antonio said. He'd always been jealous. He gave me a kiss on the cheek before we left. Sheila said I was the luckiest girl in the world. I feel like it right this minute.

Of course, Mother had to dampen my joy. She heard me and Sheila talking about him. I told her he was only four years older, that I was nearly 18 and that his band was so good they'd probably start traveling around the country soon. I didn't tell her this, but I've been thinking of traveling with the band.

Melinda's eyes grew wide. She'd never heard her mother say anything like on these pages. She looked around the room, past Jillian, past the darkening sky outside. But, she didn't see anything. Her mind was too full. She kept thinking about her mother's words. She didn't hear Charles come in or see him standing in the doorway of the room.

He cleared his throat three times before the girls noticed him.

"Hello," he said loudly.

Jillian immediately jumped up and turned the television off. "I was just leaving. I'll just go call my mama and I'll be gone."

Melinda quickly picked up the diary and followed Jillian to the other room. After Jillian hung up, Melinda said, "I think I'm finding some major clues."

"Girl, you are shaking, and you look like you just saw a ghost."

"I feel like I am reading about a ghost or something just as mysterious."

"What?"

"My mom is all crazy about this singer. He's from Italy. She even drank beer with him. I think the guy in the pictures is my dad."

"Calm down. I've never seen you like this."

"Jill, I think this is my dad."

Jillian leaned forward and put her hands on Melinda's shoulders.

"Don't worry. We'll find out." A car honked out front. "I gotta go for now. Maybe you better not read anymore until I can come back. You gotta stop shaking."

After Jillian left, Melinda paced back and forth in her room for a long time. Maybe Jillian was right and she shouldn't read anymore for a while. She needed to digest what she'd read today. It was so much new information. But, it made sense to her. She could have gotten her singing voice from this Johnny guy. That could be why her mother always had that sad, far-away look on her face when Melinda sang. Maybe Grandmother did have a reason to fear that her mother was drinking. She drank with Johnny. He was four years older and played in a rock band, too.

She didn't sleep well that night, waking up several times with hundreds of thoughts going through her head. When she finally got up, she decided she'd finish the diary and figure out the truth. She couldn't go another night without knowing.

Chapter 20

Brad insisted she run with him first thing Sunday morning. Her body felt tired and stiff at first, but after about 10 minutes, she loosened up and was glad he had talked her into it. He talked most of the time, and she was glad he didn't question her silence.

Inside, she quickly showered, changed and got back to reading. She couldn't wait another minute. She scanned through some boring pages. Now, she only read pages that had something important on them.

Johnny and I have been seeing each other a lot. Mother seems afraid of him when he comes over. He thinks she's funny. He thinks I'm beautiful. He tells me that all the time. He is the best kisser. We spend hours just kissing. He has an adorable cleft chin and I love running my finger over it. I know this sounds crazy after only knowing him for a few months, but I think he is the one.

Melinda's heart beat so fast and hard it felt like it was going to burst out of her chest. She touched the indention in her chin and her eyes welled up. Where was this guy now? Why hadn't she ever met him? When did he become her father? Her mother is now nearly 18 in the book. Melinda was born before her mother's 19th birthday. She quickly continued to flip through the pages for any other mention of Johnny.

Johnny and I got in a huge fight just before Valentine's Day. His band is starting to travel and I'm stuck here going to high school. I'm afraid he's going to fall in love with someone else even though he says I'm the only girl for him. He said he could prove it. I said how. He said we could get married. At first, I laughed. I thought he was joking, but I looked in his eyes and knew he wasn't.

Melinda fell back on the bed and stared up for awhile, then returned to reading.

Mother says I cannot see Johnny anymore. She says he is too old, and that she has smelled beer on my breath for the last time. I've only had a few sips, but she doesn't believe me. She thinks I should be going to alcohol rehab. She is becoming a real problem. She doesn't believe anything I say. I'm grounded all the time. She's driving me crazy. She's says I'm driving her crazy.

Melinda turned over on her stomach and searched through the pages for more mention of Johnny. She started to get frustrated. What happened next? Finally, she spotted Antonio's name.

Antonio came all the way from Southern Italy to visit Chicago. He stayed with us while he visited colleges here. He wants to go to Northwestern. He wants to be a doctor. Mother says, "Now there's a nice, intelligent young man, nothing like his brother." Antonio is nice. I told him everything. He's the only one who knows how Johnny and I got married on Valentine's Day, two days after my 18th birthday, about our romantic weekend honeymoon downtown and how Johnny left the next week to tour with the band. He knows how I'm staying here until I graduate in May. Then how I thought I heard giggling in the background when Johnny called last week. Antonio is worried about me. He's a good listener and friend.

Melinda couldn't believe what she was reading. She knew nothing of this. How could her mother not tell her she was married? It was obvious that Glory and Brandy Lee and her mother's family didn't know either. How could she keep such a big secret? Several pages were stuck and Melinda had to pry them apart. She read them as fast as her eyes could go.

Oh God. I'm pregnant and Johnny and I are separated. Since he started touring, it's been miserable. Every time I call his hotel room, there are always girls there. He says they are friends of the other band members. We got in a huge fight and I said this wasn't working out. I wanted him to come back to Chicago, but he said he needs to keep touring, it's all he has ever wanted in life. I said what about me. He hasn't seen me in two months. He said I need to finish school first. I said I didn't want to tour all the time. Why couldn't we get a nice bungalow on a beach somewhere? He could still be in a band. I was afraid to tell him I was pregnant already, but I said someday we will have a family. We can't travel forever. He said, you're not talking about kids already are you? He was angry and I was angry so I hung up.

Melinda's eyes welled up. She had to blink a couple of times to clear them and be able to continue reading.

My whole world has turned upside down. Just when I thought it couldn't get worse it did. I'm writing this in between throwing up and no one even knows I'm pregnant. No one. I'm having a hard time thinking. Two days ago after graduation, Sheila and Antonio (he was visiting again) and I went to celebrate. They had a few drinks. I didn't have a drop. No one understood why, but me. No one guessed I was pregnant. On the way home, I was the designated driver. I don't even know what happened. The road was curvy. I was driving too fast maybe. Mother says I must have been. I can't remember. We were laughing and talking. Next thing I knew we were off the road. The car turned over. I passed out. When I came to, they told me everyone but me was killed, but me. Somehow, I was fine. But I want to be dead. Sheila and Antonio are gone and it's my fault. Mother told everyone I had a drinking problem. I'm too embarrassed and ashamed to go to the funeral. I'm leaving tomorrow on a bus before anyone wakes up. I'll never drive again. I don't know where I'll go. Maybe west. I'm not telling anyone. Me and my baby will start our own life somehow, somewhere.

Tears rolled down Melinda's cheeks. Her mother carried so many secrets, such a heavy load for a young girl, all alone.

Chapter 21

The first day after Melinda finished the diary, she stayed home from school. She didn't shower or even get out of bed until noon. Her stomach felt like it was doubling over inside. She roamed around the house. It was still and quiet. All she could hear was the rumbling of an occasional car passing outside.

On the bottom shelf in Charles' office, she found an old family photo album. She flipped through the pages staring at pictures of her mother as a small girl. She looked happy. She was wearing a cowgirl outfit standing in front of a Christmas tree. In another picture, she had her arm around a tall snowman with a carrot nose and dark round eyes. On another page, she and Charles were waving from a roller coaster seat. And in another, the whole family sat arm and arm at a restaurant with balloons and a cake on the table.

The telephone rang throughout the day, but Melinda didn't answer it. When Charles came home around 9 p.m., she listened to him in the kitchen, to the click of his shiny black shoes as he walked across the wood floor and then to the shutting office door. She started to doze off, but was awakened by Charles knocking on her door.

"Melinda, are you in there?"

"Yes," she said.

"There were several messages on the answering machine. The school wondering where you were today. Jillian asking about a diary or something, and Glory wondering why you didn't stop by after practice."

"I stayed home today. I was kind of sick."

"Are you better? Do you need anything?"

"No thanks. I'll go to school tomorrow."

• • •

At first Melinda felt like she lost her mother all over again. It took her a few days to get over the shock. She told Glory and her friends, and then she called Darcy and told her everything. Darcy cried on the telephone and said she couldn't wait to see her in two weeks.

To Charles, Melinda left a note. She briefly explained what she'd learned and asked if he, being a lawyer, could help her find a man from Italy by the name Johnny Ventura. She told him the only thing she knew about him was that he was in a band 15 years ago and he had a brother named Antonio. Each day, she watched for a return note on the kitchen counter, but after a week went by, she gave up hope.

When she told Brad one day after she had practiced with the boys' team, he kept saying, "Wow, that's deep." He encouraged her to focus on the invitational, come in first place and get her mother's name on the cross-country wall. When they ran on the weekends, he loved to say "Race you home" when they were almost to their street. He said that was one of his favorite stories about her mother.

• • •

The morning of the track meet was damp and cool. A light mist fell as Melinda walked onto the track. Five schools were invited to the invitational at Little Notre Dame. Roosevelt was one of them. Melinda scanned the crowd in the fields and on the track looking for her friends. The Trinity team in their blue and gold uniforms gathered at the far side. She slowly walked toward them. She looked up at the crowded bleachers. She felt a sudden pang of nervousness. This was her first and last invitational at Trinity. Next year, she would go to high school. She really wanted to win, to get the Overstreet name on the permanent track plaque near the gymnasium.

She took two deep breaths and closed her eyes. The moisture in the May breeze reminded her of home. She and her mother had run in drizzle like this on the Oregon coast many times. "This one's for you, Mom."

"Melinda!" Jillian ran toward her.

"Don't jump on me."

"I wasn't. I'm saving that for later, when you win. Are you ready?"

"I'm never ready to be smashed into the ground."

They both laughed. "You know that's not what I meant."

"I know." Melinda smiled.

The announcer's garbled voice blared through the speaker overhead. After the National Anthem, the meet would begin with the 50-yard dash.

"When's your event?" Melinda asked Jillian as they sat down and stretched.

"The 100 hurdles is third and the 300 hurdles is sixth." Jillian extended one leg forward and bent the other behind her. "I see your team over there. You can always tell if it's a private school. Everyone primps before they sweat. Look at Ashleigh. She's brushing her hair again."

Melinda glanced over her shoulder. Ashleigh's straight blond hair glistened even on this hazy day. Her uniform looked ironed and her bright white shoes and socks were obviously new. She fanned her fingers in front of her. Melinda imagined they had a fresh coat of nail polish. How did she always look so tan? Brad stretched in the grass with a group of guys a few feet away from Ashleigh. He'd nodded and smiled at Melinda when she'd walked past a few minutes ago.

"First call for 100 Hurdles," the speaker blared.

"Good luck, Jill," Melinda yelled as Jillian ran toward the start line.

"Oh, there you are Melinda," Coach Cox said. She pulled her coach's jacket over her head as the drizzle turned to rain. The stands became a patchwork of colored umbrellas. "Sorry about the weather. You'll be running through puddles and mud. The trails will be slippery. Be careful on that steep hill."

"I'll be fine."

"Final call for the 200 Dash," the speaker announced.

"Melinda, the team's gathering over here. Please, come join us." Coach Cox jogged toward the middle of the field.

Melinda heard Jillian's name announced for second place in the 100 Hurdles.

"All right, Jillian," Melinda yelled. To herself, she said, "Wish I could run at you and knock you down. Maybe later." She looked through the thick crowd for Jillian. On the other side of the field, she saw Emily turning and throwing the shot put. As she got near her team, Brad joined her. Runners were pacing back and forth in all directions.

Coach Cox ran up to Melinda, "They just announced first call for girl's cross country. Brad, get ready, you'll be next. Good luck, both of you."

Melinda's heart beat faster than it ever had her whole life. Her palms were sweaty and she wiped them on her damp shorts. As she jogged toward the start line, Brad ran along with her.

"Remember, 'Race You Home.' You'll do great."

At the starting line, a group of wet cross-country runners bounced on their toes, swung their arms and stretched their legs. As the rain continued to fall, the crowd screamed, "Go Maria. Go Kristi. You can do it Colleen." Melinda's heart pounded. She tilted her head from side to side to relieve the tension that had built up in her neck.

Ashleigh crowded in next to Melinda. "From now on, you stay away from Brad," she sneered. Then, she giggled, "Don't break a leg trying to catch me."

"Go get 'em, Mel." Jillian gave her a thumbs-up sign from the sideline. Melinda waved back. The announcer shouted, "Runners on your Mark, Get Set, GO." A gun sounded and the pack of runners started the three-quarters around the track. Ashleigh pulled out in front. Melinda was in the middle of the pack as they turned off the track and onto the grassy field leading to the wooded trail.

In the straight-away, Melinda passed three runners. She worked her way up to third, two spots behind Ashleigh before they reached the trees. Heavy, rhythmic breathing and the pounding of running shoes on the muddy ground filled the normally quiet woods with a rushing sound. The trees blocked some of the rain so that it came down in a drizzle beneath them. A thin layer of pine needles blanketed the running path.

Ashleigh looked over her shoulder as Melinda inched her way into second place. Melinda felt at home on the slippery trail, while the other girls struggled to keep their pace. She remembered what Brad had said about kicking forward and straightening her back. She puffed out big breaths over and over. She pushed herself. She wanted to take the lead before they cleared the woods. This is where she had the advantage. She didn't know if she could overtake Ashleigh in a straight-away. She caught up to Ashleigh. Melinda tried to pass. Ashleigh stepped to the side so Melinda couldn't. Melinda tried the other side, but Ashleigh, who kept peering over her shoulder, blocked the way again. They came to a steep hill, and Melinda knew she could pass Ashleigh. She knew she was stronger.

As they climbed the steep slope, Ashleigh's foot slipped and her pace slowed. Melinda made her move to take the lead. Ashleigh reached over, grunted and shoved Melinda with her right arm. Melinda was forced off the trail into a thick pile of brush. She stumbled forward, but regained her footing without falling. She got back on the trail a few feet behind Ashleigh. The other runners were getting closer. Melinda knew the course well. The top of the hill was the half-way point. She still had a chance to pass Ashleigh on the downhill before the clearing.

A few steps from the top, Ashleigh groaned and fell to the ground. Melinda slowed slightly, but ran past the downed runner. Melinda listened for Ashleigh to get up and start running again. When she didn't hear anything, she looked over her shoulder. Ashleigh lay in a heap with her face hidden, her long arms and legs sprawled out on the wet ground. The other runners were more than half way up the hill. If Ashleigh didn't get up soon, they'd all pass her.

Melinda stopped at the top of the hill. Her breathing was loud. She looked toward the path in front of her. She could easily win now. She'd get the Overstreet name on the wall for her mother. Everyone would be so proud to see her burst through the trees and sprint to the finish line in first place. She stared at Ashleigh's limp body. The others were now passing the collapsed runner. They each glanced down at her. "Downed runner," one of them yelled. Another one yelled behind her, "Hey, you all right?"

Ashleigh still didn't move. Melinda let out a big sigh. The runners passed her and she jogged back toward Ashleigh. She knelt down. "Ashleigh, are you okay?" Her blond ponytail curved across her cheek. Melinda moved it slightly. Ashleigh's eyes were partly open, but she was unconscious. Melinda wrapped her fingers around Ashleigh's wrist and felt a faint pulse. Her eyes darted up and down the trail, but no runners were in sight now.

She quickly stood up and ran as fast as she could toward the school, taking a short cut through the woods. She had to jump high over the thickets several times. Tree limbs and downed branches cut her bare arms and legs. She didn't care. She remembered Ashleigh throwing up in the bathroom and what the book said about collapsing and possible death. She'd heard of girls dying from bulimia and she was worried. What if it was too late? She also thought of her mother lying on the side of the road after the car hit her. What if someone could have gotten her help sooner? She darted from the woods into the clearing, nowhere near the beginning or ending of the wooded cross-country trail. As she got closer to the crowd, several people ran toward her. They had panic written all over their faces. Melinda guessed she did too.

"Coach! Coach!" Melinda yelled, almost breathless.

"What's going on, Melinda?" Coach Cox said. The other coaches and several track members were right behind her.

"She's down. She's not moving. She's unconscious." Melinda's whole body heaved up and down as she talked. She was pointing at the woods. "She's on top of the hill."

"Who? Who's down?"

"Ashleigh. Hurry. She needs help fast." Melinda bent over and held her right hand on her side where she felt a piercing pain. Her back arched up and down. When she raised her head, the coach and several other adults were jogging into the trees. Another coach was screaming, "Call an ambulance." A few minutes later, Melinda heard sirens.

She sat down on the ground and put her knees to her chest. She wrapped her arms around her legs. Her body was starting to cool off and she was getting chilled. The rain had stopped but a breeze blew the cool spring air over her body.

Jillian came up and sat beside her. She put her arm around Melinda's shoulder.

"Guess I won't ever get the Overstreet name on the running wall at Trinity," Melinda said without looking up.

"Yeah," Jillian said. "But, look on the bright side. I won't jump on you and knock you down. And, there's always next year at Marquette High School."

Melinda tried to smile.

"You did the right thing, girlfriend. I don't know if I could have done the same thing for her."

The ambulance waited at the entrance to the wooded trail. Several men placed the stretcher in the back, and the siren blared again as the vehicle sped down the road.

Jillian helped Melinda up and they walked toward the bleachers. Brad patted her on the back and smiled. Melinda searched the crowd until she found Glory, who stood up and started clapping. People around Glory did the same, Brandy Lee, Mr. Jones, Mr. Rutherford and within a few seconds, Melinda was the recipient of a standing ovation.

Chapter 22

Melinda was a hero at school the next week. Suddenly, she had many friends at Trinity. The Spring Sing was only a few days away and Melinda turned her attention to the musical event. She had been chosen to do a solo. After much discussion with Mrs. Doyle, they decided she could sing one of her mother's favorite songs from the Carole King "Tapestry" album. Melinda almost choked up the first couple of times she rehearsed it, but she sang it with such feeling that Mrs. Doyle said it would be one of the highlights of the concert.

Mrs. Doyle's excitement about the concert was contagious. Alita was to take turns playing the piano with a boy from the group, and she and Melinda were pleased when Mrs. Doyle said Alita could accompany Melinda during her solo. Mrs. Doyle always fluttered around the auditorium making sure everyone was standing in just the right spot, then she'd hurry to the back to see "how their sound was blending together."

One day, Mrs. Doyle rushed into the practice "with big news." A music professor and choir director from a university in Southwestern Michigan had agreed to come help with their final rehearsal Thursday night. She said he was excellent and the students always learned so much from him.

After choir practice, two girls told Melinda and Alita that their older sisters had said the professor was handsome and charming and they couldn't wait to meet him too.

Alita said, "I heard he was older than Mrs. Doyle."

"Who cares?" One of the girls said. "He can still be cute. Look at some of the most famous actors. They're in their 30's, too."

Melinda and Alita smiled at each other and shrugged their shoulders.

• • •

With all that was going on, Melinda most looked forward to seeing Darcy again. Her friend was flying for the first time in her life. She'd arrive Friday afternoon, take her first taxi and then make it just in time for the Spring Sing. Melinda knew Darcy would especially like the song she had chosen. They had all three sung it together many times.

Thursday afternoon, the first thing Melinda heard when she opened the door to her room was the sound of Priscilla's high-pitched voice.

"Oh, Charles, please rub my feet. I've had a long day of standing on these high heels. Charles? You're not even paying attention to me. Charles!"

"Quit yelling at me."

Melinda quietly shut the door and crept up the stairs very slowly, trying not to squeak the wooden steps. She could still hear them squabbling in the living room below.

"Charles, you are right. This relationship is not working out. Why are you always shaking your head at me like I'm some dumb schoolgirl? I am a professional business woman and I demand respect."

Melinda was almost to the top. She stopped. Priscilla was at the bottom leaning over putting her high heel shoes back on next to the front door.

"Okay, Charles. This is it. I won't call you again. If you are ever interested in this relationship again, you call me." She slammed the door and was gone.

Before Melinda could move, Charles appeared below and said, "Good riddance," to the door. He chuckled to himself as Priscilla peeled out of the driveway and sped away. He brushed his palms together in big swipes like he was ridding them of crumbs. When he turned around, he saw Melinda standing at the top of the stairs frozen with one arm on the rail and one foot in front of the other.

"Oh, hello," he said.

"Hello," she said and then walked into her room.

• • •

After sitting for a few minutes, Melinda felt too antsy to wait at home for rehearsal. She didn't see Charles downstairs so she left a note for him on the counter. She pulled her bike out of the garage and rode the few miles to Glory's apartment.

She knocked on the door several times. No one answered so she put her ear up to the door. She was sure she heard the television on, and knew that Glory had to be home. After knocking again, she walked between the bushes and peeked through the living room window. Glory was lying on the couch. Melinda banged on the window. Glory didn't move.

Melinda quickly jumped on her bike and rode to Jillian's house. Brandy Lee answered the door.

"What is it, Melinda?"

"It's Glory. She didn't answer the door. I looked in the window and she's on the couch. I banged on the window and she didn't move. Something's wrong. She's been so sick lately. We've got to hurry."

Brandy Lee sped all the way to the apartment. She had a key and unlocked the door.

"Call 911," she yelled. Melinda grabbed the phone.

Glory was limp. Her eyes closed. Brandy Lee held her. "Oh, Mama. Oh, Mama. You're going to be okay. Oh, Lord, let her be okay."

Brandy Lee rode in the ambulance while Melinda waited for Jillian and her dad. The sight of the red flashing lights and the sound of the siren haunted Melinda's thoughts for the rest of the night. Melinda waited and paced in the emergency department waiting room with Jillian's family. Finally, a doctor appeared.

He explained that Glory is anemic because she has a tumor in her colon that has been bleeding.

"What does that mean, Mama?" Jillian said in tears. Brandy Lee wrapped her arms around her daughter and they stood staring at the man who was still in pale blue surgical scrubs.

The doctor looked at the pair. "She's lost a lot of blood and we're giving her transfusions. When she's stable, which should be tomorrow, we'll take her to surgery to remove the tumor. On the CAT scan, it looked like it hadn't spread, but we won't know for sure until after the surgery tomorrow."

Jillian's dad asked him a few more questions, and then everyone agreed to come back first thing in the morning.

• • •

Melinda found Charles waiting up in the living room. He looked tired, but worried.

"Where have you been?"

"I'm sorry I forgot to call. Glory's in the hospital. She passed out, and I had to call an ambulance. She has a tumor."

All the color drained from Charles' face and his head dropped forward.

"Is she going to be okay?"

"The doctor said he'd know more tomorrow after the surgery."

Charles looked up and his eyes met Melinda's. His hair was ruffled and his whole face looked like it was sagging.

"You got a phone call about rehearsal tonight."

"Oh, my, gosh. I forgot all about that. And Mrs. Doyle was so excited for us to meet this college choir director." She let out a big sigh. "Oh, well. I'm tired. I'm going to sleep."

"Goodnight."

"Goodnight."

Melinda walked toward the stairs and Charles went the opposite way, down the hall toward his room.

• • •

When Melinda first woke up Friday morning, she thought about skipping school and going to visit Glory instead. Brandy Lee stopped by on her way to the hospital and told her she knew what she was thinking.

"You need to go today," she said. "You have the Spring Sing tonight and I know Mama wouldn't want you to miss that. She'll be fine and you'll be telling her all about the concert soon. If you don't go, you'll have to tell her you missed it. And, you know how disappointed she'd be."

When Melinda didn't answer, Brandy Lee continued, "Jillian is going to school, too. And, your friend Darcy is coming today. If you don't go to school, you can't participate in the concert. Go do it for us all, Melinda."

In the end, Melinda decided it was best. She ate breakfast and unfolded a note from Charles.

Melinda,

Sorry I forgot to tell you this last night. I'm working on tracing that name you gave me. My office has found the name John Vensura in New York, California, New Mexico, Texas and Michigan. We'll keep working on it.

Charles

At lunch, Alita told Melinda all about the college choir director. She said he was handsome, and he had a very charming personality. She said she overheard Mrs. Doyle telling him that she didn't know why Melinda didn't make it to the rehearsal, but that she'd be fine without the extra practice. She was the best singer at Trinity.

• • •

After school, Melinda rode her bike as fast as she could to the hospital. She had one hour before she had to be back to school dressed for the concert. She'd decided to wear her mother's black dress again. It was waiting for her in the dressing room outside the auditorium.

Melinda gasped when she saw Glory lying in the hospital bed with tubes coming from her nose and arms. An IV pole hung at the corner of the bed. The smells reminded Melinda of the antibiotic ointment she put on scrapes and scratches. Glory's eyes were closed. Melinda walked to the side of the bed and held Glory's hand.

A tear ran down Melinda's cheek. "Don't you leave me too," she whispered.

Glory's eyes fluttered and she squeezed Melinda's hand. She tried to talk and Melinda leaned close to her mouth. "I'm not going anywhere yet," she choked out.

Melinda smiled. "You better not."

Before she left, she kissed Glory on the cheek. While she was down near her face, Glory said, "Good luck tonight."

• • •

Melinda rushed back to the school. She changed and then squeezed her way through the students to find her spot on the risers.

"There you are," Mrs. Doyle said as Melinda flew past her straightening her dress. "You were beginning to worry me. You're here. That's the important thing."

A spotlight went to the middle of the stage, the audience grew still and Mrs. Doyle took the microphone and walked to the front.

"Welcome everyone. The eighth grade students of Trinity are proud to present the annual Spring Sing. As you can see in your programs, we will sing most of the numbers together. We will also have three solos by three very talented students. I'd like to thank Mr. John Vensura for assisting us with our dress rehearsal last night. We feel very honored to have a person of his musical caliber volunteer his time and expertise."

Mrs. Doyle started clapping and the audience joined her.

Melinda's eyes were darting all over the room. She could see a light was shining in the front row, and she knew it must be on John Vensura, but she could not see him from her position in the risers.

The choir had begun to sing. She mouthed the words. She couldn't remember any of the songs. She had to get her thoughts in order, or she would not be able to perform her solo. What was the name of her solo? She couldn't even remember that. She continued to look out at the crowd. She could make out a few details of those sitting in the front row, but didn't see anyone who looked like the pictures in the secret room.

At intermission, Melinda found Alita in the crowd in the hall.

"What does he look like?"

"Who?"

"John Ventura."

"He's got thick, dark hair. It's long too. He wears it back in a ponytail. Cool, huh? He smiles all the time, and, oh, he has a big indention right here in the middle of his chin. Oh my gawd. It's the same name. The one from your mom's . . ."

"Melinda, baby," someone screamed.

Melinda quickly turned toward the voice. It was Darcy. She was thinner and looked much different. But, when she hugged her, Melinda knew she was the old friend. Darcy was crying and apologizing for being late.

"I can't get over how much you've grown." Darcy was standing back now and looking at Melinda. "You've grown into a young lady." The overhead lights flickered.

"I guess that means I better get back to my seat," Darcy said. "It's so good to be here. You'll have to show me everything." She reached into her purse. "I found this. I don't know if it means anything, but maybe." She held out a photograph of her mother cheek-to-cheek with a young man with black hair and a cleft chin. "Cute, uh? Looks Spanish to me."

"Italian," Melinda said under her breath. The lights flickered again.

"Sing your heart out, baby. I love what you're singing." She winked at Melinda. "*Home Again* was always one of my favorites on that album."

Home Again. Melinda was glad Darcy said the name of the song. She hummed the tune as she found her place back in the risers. Hers was the last solo. When Mrs. Doyle announced her name, Melinda started to make her way to the middle of the stage. As she did, Mrs. Doyle smiled and began talking. Mrs. Doyle held out her hand and Melinda took it.

"Melinda is special to us at Trinity. Her mother Carole was in my graduating class. She moved to Oregon right after graduation. She tragically left our world last year, but what she left behind is a beautiful, talented young woman whose strength is an inspiration to us all. We're glad she's come home again. So here we have a moving rendition of Carole King's *Home Again.* Welcome Melinda Overstreet." Mrs. Doyle held Melinda's hand in the air, and then the entire audience applauded with Mrs. Doyle.

Melinda felt her knees go weak. The music started and Mrs. Doyle exited the stage. Melinda took a deep breath. She didn't know if she could do this now. She hoped she could remember the first words and that the rest of the words would follow. She glanced at Alita who gave her a big smile. Alita nodded the signal to begin, and Melinda opened her mouth.

"I won't be happy 'til I'm home again," she began. The words for the entire song followed like magic. While Alita played the piano, Melinda closed her eyes and saw her mother's smiling face. The sad, far-away look was gone. Melinda belted out the song with all her heart. When she finished, she received a standing ovation. Mrs.

Doyle thanked everyone for coming and the lights came up.

Melinda saw John Ventura standing in the front row, staring at her.

They slowly walked toward each other. All of the noises around them became muddled. Their eyes locked until they stood face to face.

"Are you related to Carole Overstreet?

"Yes," Melinda answered. "She was my mother."

Johnny looked down.

"I'm so sorry to hear about her death." When he looked up, his eyes were filled with tears. "Did you know she and I were married?"

"I just found out recently," Melinda said softly.

They stared at each other for a long time. He seemed to be taking in every feature on her face.

"How old are you?" he asked.

"Almost 15."

He started to tremble. "Do you have a dad around?" He looked from side to side as if searching for someone.

"I didn't growing up," Melinda said slowly. "But, I just recently found out that I do have a dad."

Johnny lifted his hand and tapped his chest, giving Melinda a questioning look.

Now, her eyes welled up and she nodded her head.

His lips quivered as he smiled.

They embraced and laughed and cried, then laughed again.

Darcy, Brandy Lee, Jillian, Emily and Alita formed a circle around them. Jake and Sam broke away from Charles and pushed their way through.

"Why won't that man let go of Melinda?" they said turning back to their father.

"He's your uncle, boys, and Melinda's dad."

Chapter 23

At first, Melinda and her father were surrounded by family and friends, but slowly everyone went home and left them alone. He laughed when Melinda told him stories about growing up. He cried when she told him about her mother's accident. He described his life since his brother's death and his young wife's sudden departure. Johnny had been devastated. His parents talked him into returning to Italy. After a couple years, he went back to school and studied music. He taught in Southern Italy before returning to this area. He was attracted to a Michigan resort town and settled there. He volunteered to help at Trinity each year in the hope of learning something about Carole. He'd had no idea he was a father. He wanted to make up for all the lost time. His eyes spoke louder than his words.

• • •

The first week of June, Melinda walked alone through the cemetery. She placed flowers on the top of the gravestone and knelt on the fresh dirt before it. She lowered her head.

"I don't know where to start," she whispered. "I love you and I miss you. I'm glad I came here, to your city, your school and your house. I understand everything better now. At first, I was mad at Mom for not telling me everything. Then, I was sad for her. I thought she must have been so unhappy, so lonely. Then, I saw the pictures. They showed the good times. I know they were real, just as real as the happy times in her diary and the happy times she and I had together."

Melinda looked up at her grandmother's name engraved on the stone – Victoria Carole Overstreet. Red roses bloomed in a nearby meadow. Birds sang in the tree above her. The air smelled of fresh cut grass. She almost wiped the tear from her cheek, but instead let it fall to the ground, and she smiled.

"I'm glad you and Mom are together again. And, don't worry about me. I'm going to live by the sand and the waves and the sounds of kids playing in the water again. But, this time it's in Michigan and only an hour and a half away from here. I'll visit as much as I can. I promised Glory and the twins and Jillian and Brad. Ashleigh wants to be friends, too. She said she was sorry for everything. She gave me and Alita a box of candy and invited us to a sleepover. I think Uncle Charles even wants to see me again." She chuckled to herself. "Our house is on the beach. Grand Beach reminds me of Shorewood. I feel like I'm home. It's nice to have found my dad."

She looked at her father leaning against the car. He smiled and waved. She kissed the top of the stone, and went to join him.

About the author

Tonya McGue has over 50 articles to her credit. She has specialized in issues about family life and growing up. She is also the founder of a regional parenting magazine, *Family Ties,* originally named *Family Life & Laughter.* In addition to her non-fiction work, she has published two short stories in a regional literary magazine titled *The Noun* and a poem in the Valparaiso University literary magazine *The Lighter.* Tonya has a bachelor's and a master's degree in public relations. She has worked in various public relations positions with an emphasis on writing and creating publications. She and her husband live in La Porte, Indiana with their three children.

Printed in the United States
54442LVS00001B/223-309